SAVING AMANDA

BROTHERHOOD PROTECTORS YELLOWSTONE
BOOK #3

ELLE JAMES

TWISTED PAGE INC

SAVING AMANDA

BROTHERHOOD PROTECTORS
YELLOWSTONE BOOK #3

New York Times & *USA Today*
Bestselling Author

ELLE JAMES

Dedicated to my friend Amanda, a carefree soul who can switch on "mom" mode in a nanosecond. Let's share another grand adventure!
Elle James

AUTHOR'S NOTE

Enjoy other military books by Elle James

Brotherhood Protectors Yellowstone
Saving Kyla (#1)
Saving Chelsea (#2)
Saving Amanda (#3)
Saving Liliana (#4)
Saving Breely (#5)
Saving Savvie (#6)

Visit ellejames.com for more titles and release dates
Join her newsletter at
https://ellejames.com/contact/

PROLOGUE

"MOVE!" a deep voice pierced the veil of murky shadows inside Tobi's mind.

In an attempt to clear the fog and focus on the voice's owner, he shook his head. The sudden movement caused his world to spin faster and rubbery legs to falter. "Why?" he asked, his words slurring. The sound of his voice echoed in his head, strange even to his own ears.

"Don't you remember?" the voice said. "It's the great hunt. We have to get the buffalo to the edge of the cliff. The others are waiting."

He shook his head more slowly this time. "Not making sense. What buffalo?"

"We are but a few among our ancestors. To live, we must hunt or join our ancestors and become just as extinct. Move!"

"Hold on," Tobi reached out his hands into the

darkness of the night sky. Clouds scuttled across the full moon and the blanket of stars shining down on Montana, dimming the natural light.

"I can't see straight," Tobi said, staggering forward.

"You don't need to. I'll guide you," the voice said.

"Good, because I don't know where the hell I am." Tobi stumbled forward.

"You're a great warrior. One of a dying race. Your tribe needs you to provide for them."

"I don't have a gun, a bow or even a knife."

"You don't need them to run the buffalo," the voice said. A shadowy figure moved alongside him in the darkness.

"Run the buffalo?" Tobi tried, but he couldn't comprehend what the man meant.

"Raise your hands; get them moving."

"What buffalo?" Tobi stumbled across the uneven ground. "I don't see them. I can't think. Everything is fuzzy." He squeezed his eyes shut for a second and fell to his knees.

A hand gripped his elbow and dragged him back onto his feet.

"Juss let me sleep," Tobi begged. Surely, if he took even a little nap, his sight and mind would clear.

"No time." The relentless hand on his arm urged him to remain on his feet and push forward again. "Your people will starve if we don't run the buffalo."

"They can go to the store."

"No stores. You must run the buffalo. See them?" The figure's other black-clad arm swept before them.

Tobi shook his head, causing it to spin again. "Buffaloes have been gone for a long time."

"No. You're wrong. They're here, right in front of you. Wave your arms and run toward them. You'll see."

"Want to sleep," Tobi cried. "Who are you? Why won't you let me sleep?"

"I'm the spirit of your ancestors. Your people need you to provide for them. Isn't that what you and the other Young Wolves are trying to do?"

Tobi frowned. He couldn't think straight, but the spirit spoke of the secret he'd sworn to keep. "How do you know?"

"I am a spirit," the shadow walker said. "I know what you know."

"Where am I?" Tobi's steps slowed as he stared out at the vastness of the heavens above. Stars filled the black sky, shedding enough light to bathe them in indigo blue.

When he tried to focus on the stars, they blurred and merged into a glob of light, swimming like a school of minnows in dark waters, their silvery bodies shimmering.

The hand on his arm urged him forward. "The buffalo. We must feed our people. The government doesn't care. Only the Young Wolves."

"Only the Wolves," Tobi echoed, unable to form

independent thoughts of his own. Something had seized his brain and refused to let go.

"Your people are hungry. They will die without your help."

"Hungry," Tobi said.

"Do you see the buffalo?" the spirit asked. "They're waiting for you to run them over the edge. But you have to move faster, or they will turn on you."

The spirit, holding tightly to his arm, picked up speed until he had Tobi sprinting.

"Run like the wind," the spirit shouted. "Only you can save your people. Run!"

Tobi focused on lifting one foot after the other, his feet churning up dust, his arms pumping the air. With the spirit beside him, he could do anything.

His people needed him. They were starving. They needed the buffalo to sustain their way of life.

As he powered across the rocky terrain, the spirit ran alongside him, urging him to go faster.

"Do you see them now?" the spirit shouted.

His vision alternated between blurred and extremely sensitive to the shining profusion of stars overhead. When he stared up at the stars and back to the ground in front of him, shadows swirled. They could be the buffaloes Shadow Spirit insisted were there. All he had to do was herd them to the edge where they'd fall to their deaths, and his people could harvest the meat and hides. One buffalo could feed an entire village.

His people would not starve. The Young Wolves could get out of the business of stealing from their supplier. Everyone in the group wanted out. They just couldn't figure out how to break free without becoming targets of one of the most dangerous Native American gangs in the contiguous United States.

The NA Syndicate had a reputation for eliminating those who threatened their legitimacy.

Not that any of that mattered. Not when his people would starve if he didn't herd the bison over the cliff's edge. He had yet to see the lurking bison or the cliff's brink.

He leaned forward, letting gravity pull him along, his feet moving, his arms still pumping the air.

"That's it," Spirit said. "That's how you'll conquer the world. One step at a time. One more obstacle to overcome. Feed them, and your people will follow you. Drive the buffalo over the edge. Don't stop until we have enough to sustain our people. Go! Go! Go!"

Tobi picked up speed, the hand on his arm holding him steady as he ran toward the dark shadows, the herd of buffaloes that would save his people from starvation.

He waved his hands and shouted, whooping like an Arapaho warrior of old, or at least a contributing member of the Young Wolves, bent on helping his people through hard times.

"For our people," Spirit yelled.

"For our people," Tobi echoed.

Then they were at the edge of the cliff.

Tobi dug in his heels to slow himself.

His feet slid across loose pebbles as his momentum pushed him onward.

"For your people," Spirit shouted.

Tobi pitched forward, teetering on the edge of the cliff.

Where were the buffaloes?

His vision swirled and blurred.

"Fly like the wind," Spirit urged.

Tobi tried to back away, but he couldn't.

The wind—or maybe Spirit—shoved him from behind, sending him soaring over the edge.

Tobi spread his wings and soared into the night sky.

CHAPTER 1

"I'm so glad you came to visit." Chelsea Youngblood reached across the table at Wolf Creek Diner in West Yellowstone, Montana, and took Amanda's hand. "It's been forever since we've seen each other."

Amanda nodded. "Since we hiked the Tetons after graduating from UM."

Chelsea shook her head. "Has it been that long?"

Amanda nodded. "And yet it's like not a day has gone by." She smiled at her former college roommate. "You haven't aged a day."

"You haven't either," Chelsea said.

"How are your wolves?" Amanda asked.

Chelsea's face lit up. "Better than ever. If I can keep the ranchers from shooting them, they have half a chance at long, natural lives in the park." Her eyebrows dipped. "How is your job working with people? Are you still working with the Montana State Child Protective Services?"

Amanda sighed. "No. I've moved to Wyoming."

Chelsea's eyebrows winged upward. "That's new. I thought working with foster children was your dream job."

"It was, and I felt like I was helping." Amanda glanced away.

"Then why did you leave it?"

She met Chelsea's gaze. "There were others doing the same job I was. I got a call from an organization that practically begged me to come work with them. Their only counselor got pregnant and went home to Ohio. They were desperate. I couldn't say no."

Chelsea grinned. "It's nice to be so sought-after."

Amanda nodded. "The call came from my former foster parent. The man who set me on the path to get my college degree and to go on to become certified in counseling. How could I say no?"

Chelsea chuckled. "How is Joe?"

Her lips twisting into a wry grin, Chelsea answered, "Still alive and kicking ass, but he's way understaffed."

"That has to be a huge burden for the Chief of Tribal Police." Chelsea squeezed Amanda's hand and let go. "So, you went back to the rez."

Amanda's lips pressed together. "I did."

"And how is that working for you?"

She sighed. "I think I'm in way over my head."

Chelsea's eyebrows dipped. "Why? You're the best counselor to graduate from the University of Montana. There's nothing you can't do. You'll always make a difference."

Amanda's heart swelled at her friend's words. "I needed this," she said. "I needed someone to tell me I'm doing the right thing."

Chelsea snorted. "When have you ever done anything that wasn't the right thing? You're the rule-follower."

"Because Joe made me one." Amanda smiled at her friend. "And you were the rebel."

"Someone had to be." Chelsea sat back in her seat. "So, spill. What's shaking your confidence? Start at the beginning with where you've landed."

With a deep breath, Amanda dove in. "I'm working with teens on the Wind River Reservation about two hours from here."

Chelsea's eyes widened, and she let out a low whistle. "I don't think you could've chosen a harder job unless you were counseling teens in the gang-ridden streets of Chicago."

Amanda drew in a deep breath. "I have to admit, I almost changed my mind a dozen times driving there the first day. My feet were so cold I was ready to run."

"Why didn't you?" Chelsea held up a hand. "No, wait. You're Amanda. When you commit to something, you don't back down."

Amanda snorted. "That's me."

"I can imagine a dozen reasons why you've had second thoughts," Chelsea said. "Things can get rough on the Rez. I've heard things are pretty bad there."

"They were bad when Joe brought me home, back when I was sixteen." Amanda's lips twisted. "Bad doesn't begin to describe how things are now."

Chelsea shook her head. "Then why don't you leave?"

"As bad as it is, there are people who don't deserve to be forgotten. Not everyone on the reservation is corrupt or evil. There are a lot of good people caught up in a bad situation." Amanda smiled. "Tara Running Fox is one of them. Seventeen years old and a true old soul. I don't think she ever got the chance to be a child."

"Happens too often," Chelsea said. "I'm sure you run into some tough cases."

Amanda nodded.

"Tara and her twin brother were raised by their mother. Their father wrapped his truck around a tree when Tara was only a baby, which was probably just as well. He was an alcoholic and abusive toward their mother. When he died, it was a relief to the entire family. But it made it more challenging for their mother to put food on the table, pay the utilities and get the kids an education."

"What's troubling her besides life on the reservation?" Chelsea asked.

Amanda's back stiffened, and she sat up straighter. "Tara's twin committed suicide two days ago."

Chelsea sat still, her gaze on Amanda. "I'm sorry to hear that. How's Tara taking it? It's hard enough to lose a brother…but a twin?"

Amanda's heart pinched in her chest. "All her mother wanted was to give her children the best start they could get in life. But she had to work two jobs to do it—cleaning rooms at a hotel and working as a waitress at the casino."

"Which means she was never home," Chelsea concluded.

"Exactly." Amanda glanced out the window of the diner. "Tara and her twin Tobi pretty much raised the younger two children."

"Was the responsibility more than Tobi could handle?" Chelsea asked.

Amanda shrugged. "I don't know. I hadn't worked with him one-on-one. Tara came to me after his death for grief counseling. She can't accept that he killed himself."

"How did he die?"

Amanda looked at her friend. "He jumped off a cliff."

"Damn." Chelsea shook her head.

"Tara said he was afraid of heights. He would never have come close to the edge."

"Does she think someone pushed him?"

Again, Amanda shrugged. "Joe conducted an investigation of the scene and found nothing. He sent the body off to the medical examiner and is waiting for the results of an autopsy."

Chelsea met Amanda's gaze. "Do you think it was suicide?"

"I probably would've accepted it as suicide, except there have been two other deaths in the past few weeks. Both deemed suicides. Both friends of Tara and Tobi's."

"Sometimes, a suicide can create a contagion effect, especially among teen peer groups," Chelsea said.

"That's what I was afraid of. I was glad Tara came to me for grief counseling."

"Did the others jump off cliffs?" Chelsea asked.

Amanda shook her head. "Allison Sitting Dog, aged eighteen, jumped off the bridge over the Little Wind River, landing on the rocks below. Ryan Gray Feather, a seventeen-year-old, waded into Boyson Reservoir and drowned. I'd heard from Joe that both had high concentrations of methamphetamines in their systems when they died."

Chelsea's brow puckered. "Did Tara say anything about drugs?"

"I asked her if Tobi had been using. She said he

never touched the stuff. And he didn't drink alcohol. She said he was afraid he'd end up like his father. He didn't want to burden their mother with that kind of behavior."

Amanda could still see the fire in Tara's eyes when Amanda had asked if Tobi had been on drugs. They'd been through enough when their father had been under the influence of alcohol. The man hadn't cared who he'd hit. Tara had shown her some of the scars she bore from where he'd slammed her against a door or thrown her across the room.

Her chest tightened whenever she thought about someone punching a child or throwing one around like so much garbage. She'd been the recipient of her father's anger too often. Her mother hadn't been able to stop him. Any time she'd tried, he'd knocked her out. Eventually, she'd given up, dropped her only daughter at the police station in Casper and disappeared. Amanda had been eleven.

The state of Wyoming had attempted to rehome her with her father, who'd refused to take responsibility for his only daughter. Thus, she'd spent the next five years living in a number of foster homes.

As much as she'd disliked being hit, she'd hated living with people who'd tolerated her existence for the money the state gave them to house and feed her. When she'd gotten tired of a foster family, she'd acted up and they'd moved her to a different, equally dismal home. By the time she'd turned sixteen, she'd

been well on her way to becoming a juvenile delin-
quent, skipping school, hanging out with druggies
and gang members.

That's when Joe Sharp Spear had appeared to take
her back to the reservation where she'd been born.
Her father had died weeks before of liver failure
from drinking so heavily. On his deathbed, he'd
confessed to Joe that he'd regretted abandoning his
daughter.

Joe had made it his mission to find her and bring
her home.

Being former Special Forces and the tribal police
chief, he didn't tolerate bad behavior. He'd made
quick work of setting her onto the right path. He'd
spent nights helping her with her homework and
making sure she was successful in school.

She hadn't been able to get away with any infrac-
tions against laws or his own set of rules. Joe had
known everyone on the reservation, and they'd
reported back to him. Though he'd been strict, he'd
never raised a hand to her. Joe had shown her more
love in the two years she'd had left in high school
than she'd been given the first sixteen years of her
life.

She couldn't say no to Joe when he'd called for
help.

Chelsea leaned back in her seat and crossed her
arms over her chest. "So, is that why you came all this
way to see me?" She cocked an eyebrow.

Heat rose up Amanda's neck and into her cheeks. "I'm sorry. I'd like to say I came up only to visit with you, but that would be a lie. As it is, I feel anxious to get back on the road to Fort Washakie. I'm afraid another teen will die if I don't get back before night-fall." She gave a mirthless laugh. "It's not like we're losing a teen a day, but damn it…we've lost three in as many weeks. Who will be next?"

Chelsea patted Amanda's hand on the table. "Hey, I'm not judging. The road goes both ways. I imagine we're both so busy in our own lives and careers, neither of us really has time to just come for a visit."

"Thank you for understanding." Amanda gave Chelsea a weak smile. "You know I love you."

"And I love you, too. Best roommate I've ever had." She laid her palms on the table. "What can I do to help?"

Amanda drew in a deep breath and let it out slowly. "Last time we talked, you said you were dating a man who was prior military, then a merce-nary and who now works for a private security firm?"

Chelsea grinned. "Benjamin is a former Navy SEAL, and yes, he was a mercenary working in Afghanistan when he left the Navy. Now, he works for the Brotherhood Protectors. He's on assignment now to provide personal security for a movie star." Her smile softened. "He's amazing. I was his first assignment. Ben saved my life."

Amanda smiled. "He must be pretty great for you to fall in love with him."

"He is the best thing that's ever happened to me," Chelsea said. "Is that what you want? Are you feeling threatened and need someone for protection?"

Amanda ran a hand through her hair. "I don't want anyone on the reservation to know I'm looking into the deaths. I need someone to run interference or provide me with a good excuse to be all over the place without rousing suspicion. If the deaths aren't suicide, someone is drugging the teens and then giving them a little help over the edge."

"You need one of the Brotherhood Protectors to work your case with you."

"I don't have a lot of money." Amanda laughed. "You know how little money the Shoshone and Arapahoe have to spend on what they might consider frivolous."

Chelsea leaned over the tabletop and covered Amanda's hand with her own. "Sweetie, if these aren't suicides, you have a bigger problem. I can't imagine anyone letting you have free reign and access to every place on the reservation without rousing suspicion. You need someone to help you look and to protect you while you do."

"I hate even asking," Amanda said. "I could be imagining things."

Chelsea's lips firmed into a straight line. "Or not. Better to be safe than dead."

"That's why I came," Amanda said. "I was hoping your man could help."

"He can't." Chelsea grinned. "But I know there are others who have yet to be assigned. You need to come over to the lodge. I'll introduce you to their boss, and you can take it from there."

Amanda let go of a breath she hadn't realized she'd been holding.

"I have to run by the grocery store for a few things before I head to the lodge," Chelsea said. "You can ride with me to the store or drive your car to the lodge, and I'll be there shortly."

"I'll drive to the resort," Amanda said. "I'll wait in my SUV until you get there."

"Oh, you don't have to wait on me. You can go on in. I'll call ahead and let their boss, Stone Jacobs, know you're on your way."

Amanda regretted saying she'd go to the lodge ahead of Chelsea. But now that she'd committed, she'd suck it up and keep moving. "Thank you." Besides, the sooner she returned to Fort Washakie, the better. She was really worried about Tara and other young members of the community.

Chelsea waved to the waitress, who came over with the bill.

Amanda dug out her wallet and extracted enough money to pay for the entire meal.

Chelsea held up her hand. "I've got this."

"I complain about the pay, but I'm not destitute," Amanda said.

"You can get the drinks next time." Chelsea dropped bills onto the table and stood.

"Thank you. I hate to be in a rush, but I need to get things settled and then get back on the road."

Chelsea nodded. "I'll hurry with what I have to do and meet you there in ten minutes. Remember to ask for Stone Jacobs. He's in charge of this division of the Brotherhood Protectors."

Amanda frowned. "There's more than one division?"

Chelsea nodded. "The original agency is based in Eagle Rock, Montana. Hank Patterson is the Navy SEAL who started it. He's also set up an office in Colorado."

"Is there that much of a need for bodyguards and security agents?" Amanda asked.

"More than I could ever have imagined," Chelsea said. "And they do a lot of work pro bono."

"I can pay. I have some money saved back." Amanda had been saving money from the day she'd gotten her first job, determined never to be hungry again.

"Stone will work with you on that. Go." Chelsea shooed Amanda ahead of her. "Get to the lodge. I'll call and let them know you're coming."

Amanda turned and hugged her friend. "Thank you."

Chelsea hugged her back. "I'd go myself, but I might just get in the way. Besides, you know me, I'm better with animals than with people."

"The hell you are," Amanda smiled. "You're perfect with me."

"Yeah, and how many times have I been to see you since college?" She snorted. "Some friend, huh?"

"We've both been busy with our own lives," Amanda said. "I'm just glad we've stayed in touch by text."

Chelsea gave her the directions. "You can't miss it. There aren't a lot of streets in this little town."

Amanda headed for the exit and stepped out into the bright Montana sunshine. Already, the bright orb had passed its peak and was descending toward the western horizon.

She climbed into her SUV and drove out of the parking lot.

In her rearview mirror, she noted Chelsea heading in the opposite direction, her cell phone balanced between her shoulder and cheek.

Eager to be back on the road to Fort Washakie, Amanda drove through the streets, following Chelsea's instructions, her foot heavy on the accelerator. The sooner she got there, the sooner she'd be on her way back. With some help, she hoped to keep from losing another teen on her watch.

19

CHAPTER 2

"You must have a death wish." John Jacobs, the owner of the Grand Yellowstone lodge, stood outside the corral with his booted foot perched on the bottom fence rail.

"Why do you say that?" Carter Manning asked, keeping his tone even and soothing as he lunged the black gelding at the end of the lead. On the horse's back was a saddle, just waiting for someone to fill.

John shook his head. "He won't let you ride him out of that pen. And what goes up must come down." The older man rubbed the back of his neck. "And hard. I'm getting too old to deal with cantankerous horses. I like where my bones are and don't relish having them rearranged."

Carter chuckled. What he'd learned about John was there weren't too many things he couldn't or wouldn't do. The former Marine had set an excellent example for his son, Stone, who'd joined the Navy and worked his way through BUD/S training alongside Carter to become a Navy SEAL. They were made of tough stock and had worked hard for what they had. He respected that ethic in Stone and his father and was just as willing to work hard for what he wanted as well.

He'd spent the better part of the morning just getting the horse to go around him in a circle without rearing up every two seconds.

Diablo was aptly named. From what John had said, the horse came from the best bloodlines. However, he was stubborn, ornery and threw every rider who attempted to mount and ride him out of the corral.

What Diablo didn't know was that Carter Manning was even more stubborn and would work the beast until he got the cooperation necessary for the animal to become a good riding horse.

Carter refused to give up and refused to let the beautiful animal be sold at auction to a kill pen where the animal would be sold for its meat. Not that John Jacobs had said that's what he'd do with Diablo. Too often, horses that were of no use to their owners were sold at auction and ended up in kill pens. Diablo deserved a better life. All he needed was patience and persistence.

Over the next hour, Carter worked on gaining Diablo's trust. Eventually, he mounted the horse and rode him around and around the corral. Hopefully, the horse would be at least a little tired by the time he opened the gate and rode him out.

John was there when he did, game to do the honors, all the while shaking his head. "The local paramedics are pretty quick at responding to a 911 emergency," he said as he held open the gate for the horse and rider to pass through. "You sure you want to do this?"

Carter nodded. "We've got this, don't we, boy?" he leaned forward and rubbed the side of Diablo's neck.

The gelding nickered, dancing sideways as he spotted the open gate.

Carter forced himself to relax as the horse's energy kicked into high gear. Diablo had a thing for exiting the barnyard and leaving his rider behind when he did.

Having been born and raised in rural Texas, where every able-bodied boy learned to ride before he learned to walk, Carter was up for the challenge. Before joining the Navy, he'd ridden broncs in several rodeos, scoring shiny belt buckles and cash prizes. Granted, it had been years since he'd ridden a bucking bronc, but he was certain he could manage whatever Diablo had to give.

Maybe he was cocky, or maybe he just didn't give a damn if he was bucked off and broke his fool neck and died. Too often in the past ten years as a Navy SEAL, death had appeared to be the easier option than the missions and dangers he'd encountered. He'd charged head-first into most situations, ready to accept his fate.

Only his fate had been to live to see the next battle, the next war, the next pile of shit life had to throw at him. The worst being the loss of his wife.

Why he thought of Tracey while he was riding Diablo, he didn't know…but he did. Though his memories of her had faded, he could still see the tears in her eyes when he'd said what would be his last goodbye as he'd shipped out to Afghanistan for the sixth time.

Two months later, his commanding officer delivered the news. Tracey had been murdered in her bed by a burglar who'd thought the house was empty.

Carter had been devastated. He and Tracey had been together since grade school. They'd always known they would one day marry and have a family. They'd realized their dream of marrying, but the family part hadn't been in their cards.

Three heartbreaking miscarriages had left them sad but resolute. They'd begun looking into adoption when Carter had been deployed, yet again.

Carter found out from Tracey's parents that she had been to see her doctor that day and had learned she was two months pregnant and the baby appeared viable. She'd planned to tell him when she'd passed the three-month window, afraid to get his hopes up in case she miscarried again.

She'd never gotten the chance to tell him.

Carter had returned to the States on the next C-130 headed back. Not that he could've changed a damned thing. Tracey was gone and so was the baby she'd carried.

He couldn't help feeling that he should have been home with her. If only he hadn't stayed in the military when so many had already traded their uniforms for civilian clothes and nine-to-five jobs that meant they were home where they were needed.

If he'd been home where he should have been, Tracey would still be alive, and their baby girl would have had a chance at life.

Five years had passed since that day.

Carter had left the Navy when his enlistment was up. He'd never considered returning to their hometown where he and Tracey had grown up together. Instead, he'd joined his friend Stone Jacobs, and several other former military men, to form Stone Security Specialists. They'd hired out to companies who'd conducted business in war-torn Afghanistan.

Stone and his team made sure the people they worked for got in and out of the country safely. They'd been there to make certain the last of their clients made it out of Afghanistan when the US had pulled the plug and left the country. Though their clients made it out, Stone and his team had been trapped, lacking transport.

Hank Patterson and his Brotherhood Protectors

had flown from Montana to Afghanistan to execute their daring rescue.

He owed Hank his life. With the rules changed in Afghanistan and the country back under the control of the Taliban, Stone's team of mercenaries had found themselves out of work and targeted by the new regime.

Thankfully, Hank had more than enough work to offer them jobs with his organization. He'd assured them that he could always use the skills Stone, Carter and the others had honed during their time in the military.

So, here Carter was in Montana, trying to break a horse while he waited for his first assignment with Hank's Brotherhood Protectors. Stone's team of mercenaries had been absorbed into Hank's agency and would operate a division out of West Yellowstone.

They'd been there a few weeks, acclimating to life back in the States, waiting for their assignments. But there was only so much fishing and horseback riding Carter could do before he went batshit crazy. He couldn't stand still too long, or his past would catch up and remind him of all he'd lost. Carter had to keep moving, the faster the better.

That's when he'd decided to take on Diablo as a challenge. And if he got bucked off and broke his stupid neck, then he wouldn't have to worry about finding activities to keep him busy to fill the hours of the day with something besides regrets.

As John Jacobs had predicted, Diablo balked at the gate, dancing sideways instead of moving forward through the opening.

Carter gently nudged the horse's sides with his heels and leaned close to the animal's ears, where they lay back against his head. "It's just a gate," he whispered. "You can do it. Don't you want to stretch your legs and race like the wind?"

John chuckled. "Oh, he will, once he leaves you in the dirt."

Carter was ready. He urged Diablo forward, refusing to let him remain in the corral. He couldn't continue to stand still, and Carter was not getting off to lead him through the gate. If it was a battle of the wills Diablo wanted, a battle he'd get.

Carter turned the horse toward the gate and tapped his heels against his flanks again with a little more pressure this time.

As if he'd been jabbed with spurs, Diablo leaped forward, arched his back and came down hard enough to jolt Carter's teeth together.

Carter pitched forward, righted himself and settled back in the saddle for the ride.

Diablo bucked, pitched and spun, refusing to pass through the gate.

John slapped his cowboy hat against his jean-clad leg and hollered, "That's the way to do it. Ride him!"

Other members of Carter's team appeared beside the corral.

"Come on, Manning!" Dax Young shouted.

"Dude, you're out of your mind," Benjamin "Bubba" Yates called out. "That horse is crazy."

"Eight seconds is all you need," Moe chimed in. "We got time to place bets?"

Hunter Falcon pulled a bill out of his wallet and held it in the air. "Twenty bucks says he won't make it past the gate."

"Twenty says he'll make it past the gate, but not on the horse." Stone Jacobs grinned as he joined his father near the gate.

Tim "Tinker" Smith hurried out of the barn. "Hold on, Manning. You're already three seconds more than the last man who tried to ride that devil."

Mike "Cookie" White came running from the lodge, still wearing his signature cook's apron with a beer logo emblazoned across the bib. "Ten bucks says he'll make it," the lodge cook said, waving a ten-dollar bill above his head.

"We're already up to twenty," Dax said.

"Then twenty says he'll make it," Cookie said as he skidded to a stop at the fence rail.

Carter saw them out of the corner of his eye and heard their words, but he didn't let his concentration stray from the animal beneath him to acknowledge their presence or to place his own bet.

With every change of direction, Carter swayed,

keeping his seat throughout the horse's determined effort to toss his rider.

After several minutes of wild cavorting, Diablo must have realized he wasn't going to unseat Carter. Eventually, the bucking slowed and finally ground to a halt.

The horse breathed hard, his chest heaving, his eyes still wild and his ears pinned back.

Carter reached out and rubbed Diablo's neck. "Get it all out of your system?"

This time, when he turned toward the gate, Diablo took a step forward. Then another.

When his nose came even with the open gate, he blew out a snort like an angry bull.

Carter could feel Diablo's body tense, his muscles bunching.

Then as if flying over an obstacle, the horse leaped past the gate and took off at a mad gallop, tearing out of the barnyard and heading for the lodge.

A cheer went up behind him as Carter leaned forward and let the horse have his head. He needed to run out whatever demons plagued him. The longer and faster he ran, the more exhausted he'd become.

Diablo blew past the lodge and raced down the road, leading away from the lodge. His hooves pounded against the pavement as he ran like his life depended on getting away from the corral, the gate and the men who'd gathered to watch the rodeo.

Carter braced himself as the road came to a T intersection. He reined right, praying Diablo took the cue and angled toward the road leading out of town. The horse could go either way. Carter remained ready for anything the horse had in store for him.

Trees and bushes marked the corner, blocking their view of the road to the left.

Carter pulled back on the reins, urging Diablo to slow.

Diablo had the bit between his teeth and wasn't responding to Carter's turn signals or brakes.

They hit the turn at full gallop.

Diablo veered left toward town.

As they passed the trees and bushes, a black SUV appeared in front of them, going too fast. The driver hit the brakes. The vehicle skidded sideways and straight for them.

Diablo spun and reared back on his hind legs so fast that Carter's foot slipped out of the stirrup. He reached for the saddle horn, missed and lost his balance.

The horse landed hard on his front hooves and kicked up his hindquarters so fast Carter flew over the top of the animal's head, turning a somersault in the air before landing flat on his back on the gravel shoulder of the road.

He hit the ground so hard that air blasted from his lungs, and pain shot through the back of his skull all the way to the front. Bright stars swam before his eyes, and his head thrummed to the sound of hooves pounding the earth, racing away from where he lay, unable to move, breathe or form a single curse word.

The SUV that had been racing up the road rolled to a stop. A door opened, then closed, and footsteps tapped against the pavement.

The first thought that surfaced from the haze of fog gathering at the edge of his vision was to yell at the driver for driving too fast and recklessly. If he could get his lungs to work again, he'd do just that. As yet, he couldn't manage to suck air into his empty lungs.

A woman with dark hair and blue eyes stopped beside him, a frown furrowing her pretty brow. "Hey, mister, are you all right?" When he didn't respond right away, she dropped to her knees and placed her hand on his chest. "Talk to me."

As hard as he tried, Carter couldn't force air past his vocal cords. He didn't have any air to force, and he felt helpless, lying there, unable to speak or move.

Then his body shook free of whatever had temporarily paralyzed him. He sucked air into his lungs and let it out in a whoosh.

The woman sat back on her heels and pressed a hand to her chest. "Oh, thank God. You're alive."

"No thanks to you," he said and sat up, his vision blurring for a second.

"Me?" She pushed to her feet. "You're the one

riding out of nowhere like a bat out of hell. You're lucky I was able to stop as quickly as I did."

"You shouldn't have been driving that fast on a city street."

She crossed her arms over her chest. "You shouldn't be riding a horse on a city street where cars will drive. Especially around a blind curve. You could've gotten that poor horse killed." She looked around. "Where'd he go?" She glared at him. "Do you see what you've done? Now that poor animal could be running the streets. Any number of vehicles could hit him."

His head hurt, and his thoughts and vision weren't all that clear. But somehow, he knew he was the one in the right, not this mouthy woman who was feeling sorry for the devil himself. He staggered to his feet and wished he'd stayed seated on the ground a few minutes longer. The world tilted, and his knees buckled.

The woman rushed forward and wrapped her arm around his waist, steadying him. She reached behind her, pulled a cell phone out of her back pocket and pressed three numbers before holding the phone to her ear.

Carter frowned. "Who are you calling?"

"911," she said. "Obviously, you're not all right."

He shook his head and regretted it immediately as pain shot through his temple. "I'm fine," he insisted. "I don't need an ambulance."

"The hell you don't." She focused on the cell phone. "Sorry. I wasn't talking to you. I'd like to report an accident. A man fell off his horse, and he's not doing so well."

A spark of anger forced Carter's vision and thoughts to clear immediately. He took the phone from the woman's hand and said, "I'm fine."

"Sir, I've alerted the local fire department to send a paramedic. I just need your location."

"Cancel the call. I'm on my feet, my head is clear, and I'm telling you, I don't need a paramedic. I'm steps away from the Grand Yellowstone Lodge, where I'm staying. I'll head back there. If I need help, I'll get it myself. Thank you." He ended the call and handed the cell phone back to the woman. "Now, if you'll excuse me, I have a date with the devil."

He walked away from the woman who'd almost run over him and toward the black demon who'd taken him for one hell of a ride.

But, damn it, he'd gone past the gate before he was thrown. That was progress, right?

Diablo had found a patch of lush green grass twenty yards away from where he'd dumped Carter on the ground. As Carter approached, Diablo lifted his head, long grass dangling from between his lips.

He could swear the horse was silently laughing at him.

Carter snagged the reins and turned back toward the lodge.

The woman with the dark hair and incredibly blue eyes was climbing into the SUV. She glanced back at him before she slipped behind the wheel and turned her vehicle toward the lodge.

Even though his head ached, and he had bruises on his backside, a strange thrill of anticipation rippled through him.

Was she going to be a guest at the lodge? If so, he relished the thought of running into her and verbally sparring with her over who was at fault, the horseman or the driver.

Diablo nudged his arm, pushing him toward the lodge and the woman.

"Yeah, she almost got us. All the more reason for you to get a grip. What is it with you and gates, anyway?"

Diablo tossed his head, jerking back against the reins Carter held in his hand.

"You and I are going to rumble until we come to some kind of understanding." He looped the reins over Diablo's neck and jammed his foot into the stirrup, wincing at the parts of his body that hurt from his fall.

Diablo danced sideways.

Carter held onto the saddle horn and dragged himself up into the saddle, ready to go for another wild ride if the mood took the horse.

Once Carter settled into the saddle, Diablo stood

calmly, as if he was an angel, not the devil's namesake.

"Now, you're going to act right?" Carter leaned forward and rubbed the horse's neck. "Fine. I think we've had enough excitement for one day."

He rode back to the lodge, his gaze going to the SUV that had almost nailed him and Diablo. The vehicle stood empty. Its pretty driver must have already gone into the lodge.

Carter and Diablo skirted the lodge and headed for the barn, where the men stood talking and laughing. Stone Jacobs spotted him first. A cheer went up from his teammates.

When he slid out of the saddle to the ground, he winced.

Stone took the reins and walked with Carter toward the barn. The others fell in beside them.

"Based on the gravel in your hair and the dirt on your jeans, our boy here dumped your ass, didn't he?" Stone asked.

Carter nodded. "If we hadn't almost had a head-on collision with a vehicle on the road, we'd have been okay."

"You made it farther than anyone has so far," John Jacob said. "Here, let me take him."

Carter shook his head and took the reins from Stone. "I'll take care of him," he said. "He needs to know I'm not all bad. Brushing and feeding is the good stuff he deserves after being worked so hard."

Stone nodded. "Fair enough. See you in the lodge when you're done in the barn. Our vacation is about to end. Hank has a few things heading our way soon."

Carter nodded. "I'll be in as soon as I've settled Diablo in his stall."

Left alone in the barn with the gelding, Carter went to work, divesting Diablo of the saddle, blanket and bridle. After a thorough brushing, he led the horse into his stall and gave him a can full of grain and a couple of sections of hay.

"You did good today," he said and patted the horse's neck. "We'll do this again soon."

How soon, Carter wasn't sure. Whatever work they were assigned would take precedence over taming a stubborn horse.

Despite the bruises and aching head, Carter felt good about the day and his work with Diablo. As he headed toward the lodge, his thoughts turned to a pair of blue eyes and jet-black hair so different from his dead wife's brown eyes and sandy-blond hair. Maybe that was what he needed. Something different to take his mind off what he'd lost.

Not something, but someone.

CHAPTER 3

"HELLO?" Amanda called out as she stood in the lobby of the Grand Yellowstone Lodge.

With no one at the reception desk, the place appeared to be empty.

"Hello. Anyone here?" she called a little louder, anxious to get this meeting over with so she could get back on the road to Fort Washakie.

"I'm here," a female voice responded. A woman with hair as black as Amanda's came out of one of the doors behind the reception desk. "What can I help you with?" She smiled. "Are you checking in?"

Amanda shook her head. "I'm looking for Stone Jacobs."

The woman's smile widened. "Well, you've come to the right place. I believe he's out at the barn watching one of his guys break a horse." She tilted her head toward the rear of the building. "If you follow me, I'll show you where he is."

"Thank you." Amanda fell in step with the woman.

"By the way, I'm Kyla." The woman held out her hand. "Stone and I are…together."

Amanda took the woman's hand. "Nice to meet you. I'm Amanda Small. My friend Chelsea suggested I speak with Stone about a situation I'm facing at the Wind River Reservation in Wyoming."

Kyla gave her hand a firm shake. "Then you've come to the right man…or men. Stone and his team are good at handling situations. I doubt I'd be alive today if it hadn't been for Stone's team and the Brotherhood Protectors."

Amanda's eyebrows rose. "Really?"

The woman appeared strong and capable of taking care of herself. "What happened?"

Kyla shrugged. "I got caught in the withdrawal from Afghanistan and didn't have a ride home. They got me here and kept me safe when trouble followed me back."

Amanda would love to hear more when she had more time. The woman was interesting and pretty, in an athletic, dangerous kind of way.

"They hire out their services, right?" Amanda asked.

"Yes, they do." Kyla led her through the rear door onto a wide back porch filled with rocking chairs and a porch swing. "I'll let Stone fill you in on the details. I, for one, can vouch for their amazing skills and dedication." She glanced toward the barn. "Oh, here they come now."

A small group of broad-shouldered men crossed the yard, all talking and laughing among themselves.

The man in the middle with dark hair and flecks of gray in his sideburns looked up and grinned at Kyla. "Hey, gorgeous. You missed the show."

She returned his smile. "I watched from the window. Glad he made it back alive and intact."

"He did good. He'll be up in a few minutes." His gaze shifted to Amanda as he climbed the porch steps. "Who have you got here?"

Kyla turned to Amanda. "Amanda Small, this is Stone Jacobs." She nodded toward the man standing beside Stone, who could have been his twin in his younger days. They had the same facial structure and build. The older man's hair was liberally streaked with gray. Both men had light blue eyes. "And this is John Jacobs, Stone's father and the owner of the lodge."

Amanda shook hands with Stone and his father, then focused on Stone. "My friend Chelsea said you might be able to help me."

Stone nodded. "She called right before I came out to the barn and told me you'd be stopping by. What can we do for you?"

Amanda looked around at all the men standing nearby and hesitated. "Can we talk in private?"

Stone waved a hand around the semi-circle of men standing behind him. "We can, but these men, less the old guys, are my team. The old guys are prior military. I'd trust them with my life and yours." He faced her again. "What seems to be the problem?"

On the spot, with more than half a dozen sets of eyes on her, Amanda frowned. "I'm worried about the teens on the reservation. We've had three alleged suicides in two weeks. All teens from the same social circle."

"And you don't believe they were all suicides?

Amanda shook her head.

"The first two were ruled suicides. One jumped off a bridge. The other drowned in a lake. The third jumped off a cliff."

Stone's brow dipped low on his forehead. "What did the medical examiner have to say about causes of death?"

Amanda sighed. "The first two had high concentrations of methamphetamines in their systems. The third was taken to the medical examiner yesterday. We don't have the lab results back yet."

"No witnesses?"

"None."

A very tall man with brown hair and brown eyes stepped forward. "Meth can make people do crazy things." He held out his hand. "Hi, Amanda, I'm Benjamin Yates."

Amanda smiled and took his hand. "Bubba.

Chelsea's told me so much about you; I feel like I know you already."

He shook her hand with a firm but gentle grip. "Same."

"What exactly do you want us to do?" Stone asked.

"I'm not exactly sure," Amanda admitted. "I just don't feel like I can cover all the bases by myself. I'm afraid for the teens. I've set up a support group for kids in case the deaths of their friends give them the same ideas. I can counsel all day long, but if they're being maneuvered or forced to end their lives, no amount of counseling will save them. I need help. Or at least a second set of eyes watching what's happening."

"And that someone could also watch your back," Stone said. "If there's a killer helping these kids to their deaths, he might come after you if he thinks you'll get in his way."

Amanda frowned. "I'm more concerned about the kids. I can't stand by and do nothing."

"What is the tribal police doing about it?"

"I know the tribal police chief," Amanda said. "He's just as concerned. If they are committing suicide, the idea could continue to spread to other teens. I'm working on the counseling side of this, managing grief and helping them to come up with other options rather than taking their lives."

"But you need someone to look at the other possible cause of death." Stone nodded. "Murder."

Amanda shivered. "It has to stop. These kids are just beginning their lives." She stared up into Stone's blue eyes. "Can you help me?"

Stone nodded. "We can. We're just getting started here in this division and have been waiting for the work to begin flowing in. In fact, I just got a call from our founder that we need most of the team for a security detail at a resort in Big Sky. I'd planned on taking all of them, but I can pull one guy out to work with you in Wyoming." Stone looked at the men around him, his eyes narrowing.

Dax raised his hand. "I'd be glad to help."

Stone shook his head. "This detail is on the Wind River Reservation. They're not going to talk to a blond-haired and blue-eyed white man. No, we need someone who can blend in a little better."

Stone's gaze paused on two men with dark hair and dark eyes. "Moe or Hunter could possibly handle it, but I think…" He looked toward the barn and grinned. "No. I think Manning is the right guy for the job. And speak of the devil, he's just back from a ride with the devil."

The others turned, creating a gap between their broad shoulders.

Amanda could see all the way to the barn. A man in dusty jeans and an even dustier black T-shirt strode toward them, a cowboy hat on his head, shading his face.

Something about the way the man moved seemed

familiar, but Amanda couldn't see the man's face beneath the brim of the hat until he came abreast of the others and lifted his chin.

Her heart leaped into an erratic rhythm, and her breath caught in her throat. Amanda stopped short of saying, *You!*

He stared straight at her, his eyes narrowing. "What's going on?"

Stone grinned and clapped a hand to the man's back. "I know you've been chomping at the bit to get back to work. Well, you're about to get your first assignment with the Brotherhood Protectors."

His eyes narrowed to slits. "Doing what?"

"Helping Miss Amanda Small with a situation on the Wind River Reservation," Stone said.

"Why me?" he asked, his tone harsh and mouth tight.

Amanda bristled and turned toward Stone. "Good question. Why him?"

Stone's lips twisted into a wry grin. "Manning is like a stealth operator. He gets in quickly, assesses the lay of the land and determines the best course of action before the enemy even knows he's there. He has a way of blending in." Stone looked at the rest of the group. "Am I right?"

The other men all nodded.

All the while Stone spoke, Amanda scraped her brain for a good reason to reject Stone's choice and ask for a different man to help her with the teens.

"And Manning is good with knives," Dax said.

"My thoughts exactly," Stone said. "Which could come in handy since the tribal police might not take kindly to him carrying a gun onto the reservation."

The frown on the dusty cowboy's face couldn't be any deeper than the one Amanda could feel pushing her brow low on her forehead. She'd come for help. Stone was offering help in the shape of a man with a bit more attitude than Amanda had the time or energy to deal with. But she'd asked for help, and Stone was offering it. To reject it now would be cutting off her nose to spite her face.

Manning's gaze met hers.

Was Amanda mistaken? Did she see the man's lips quirk upward? She could swear they had, if only for a second.

His brow furrowed. "What exactly will I be doing?"

"You're to help Miss Small figure out why teens are dying," Stone said. "And keep her safe in the process."

Manning squared his shoulders and met her gaze. "When do I start?"

Stone turned to Amanda. "From what I understand, the sooner the better."

"Yes," she said.

Manning gave a brief nod. "I'd like to shower before we go. I can be ready in fifteen minutes."

"No hurry, Mr. Manning," Amanda said. "We

don't have to leave at the same time. In fact, you can follow later, or even come tomorrow."

"Are you leaving immediately?" Manning asked.

"Yes," she said. "I like to get back before dark. There are too many animals on the road after dark."

"Then I'll wait to shower until I get to where we're going. I assume I'll be staying with you…?"

Amanda frowned. "Since I'm half Arapaho, I can live on the reservation, and I do. I have a one-bedroom cottage." She shook her head. "You might be able to get a room at a hotel in Fort Washakie."

Manning shook his head. "I can't keep you safe if I'm not near enough to run interference. If you don't want me in your home, then you'll have to come with me to the hotel. Again, I can't protect you if we're miles apart."

Amanda was beginning to wish she hadn't come all the way to West Yellowstone. She wasn't sure this man could help. But hell, any help was better than doing nothing and having another teen die.

"You can sleep on my couch," she said. "I'm leaving in ten minutes with you or without."

"Will the tribes give you grief about having someone not from either the Eastern Shoshone or the Northern Arapahoe tribes living with you?" John Jacobs asked. "They might be suspicious of you bringing a white man onto the reservation."

"You could say he's a visiting friend," Dax said.

"Or a cousin from another state needing a place

to stay for a week or so," the one called Moe suggested.

"They'd give you less of a hassle if he was family, even if he's white," the older man wearing a cook's apron said.

"A one-bedroom house?" Kyla shook her head. "If he's staying with you, you'd be better off telling people he's your fiancé or husband. They can't argue with that."

Amanda's heart raced as her gaze met Manning's. What had started as a cry for help was making her even more anxious. She had to remind herself that the kids were what was important. She'd make a deal with the devil himself if it meant saving even one life.

She nodded. "We'll say Mr. Manning is my fiancé. That will keep them from questioning his presence on the reservation."

Manning's mouth quirked upward at the corners. "Your fiancé, huh?"

Lifting her chin, Amanda stared down her nose at the man. "Can you manage that, Mr. Manning?"

He nodded. "Can you?"

She straightened her shoulders. "Certainly."

"Then you might want to call me by my first name."

Amanda blinked. "It's not Manning?"

The men around them laughed.

Manning shook his head. "Call me Carter. And we'll need to work on our story to make it believable.

We should probably ride together back to the reservation and nail down the details of the mission and our engagement."

"I need my vehicle, and you'll need yours."

"We can bring your vehicle tomorrow under the pretext that it had to have work done," Stone said. "The two-hour drive back to the reservation will give you ample time to brief Carter on what's happening and come up with how you two met and got engaged."

Carter's gaze locked with Amanda's. "You came to us for help," he said. "Is this what you had in mind?"

Amanda could have said no. Should have said no. Instead, she found herself nodding. "Yes." Her eyes narrowed. "Are you sure you're up to it? You had a nasty fall from that horse. Are you right in the head?"

Again, the men around him laughed.

The man called Moe snorted. "Always knew you weren't right in the head, Manning. Seems your fiancée caught onto that pretty quickly."

John Jacobs grinned. "Figures Diablo would dump you in front of a witness. That bastard likes to put on a show."

"How hard was that fall?" Stone asked.

"I'm fine," Carter said. "Been through worse shakeups in the sandbox."

Stone stared at Carter a moment longer before nodding. "I'll notify Hank of your assignment. Remember you can use his computer guy to track down information. Swede's good at getting to data. Use him."

"I've got their numbers in my cell phone," Carter said.

"You might not have heard what I told the others," Stone said. "The rest of us will be working a security detail for a resort at Big Sky while you're down at Wind River. If you need backup, I can pull someone back or ask Hank for support. Don't wait too long to ask for help."

Carter nodded.

Stone gripped Carter's hand and gave it a firm shake. "Good luck. Or should I say break a leg?" He tipped his head toward the lodge. "Grab your go bag, Carter. You have a mission."

After Carter entered the lodge, Amanda drew a deep breath and let it out slowly.

For better or worse, she was returning to the reservation with a brand-new fiancé, the stranger who'd almost crashed his horse into her car. The jury was still out on whether this was a good idea or a big mistake.

CHAPTER 4

Carter took less than five minutes to shove all his worldly goods into his duffel bag.

He didn't have much, having donated his household goods to a local shelter after losing his wife and unborn baby. Things didn't mean much to him, and life had become an endless progression of days and nights, pushing through with no real purpose other than to support his team.

Slinging his duffel bag over his shoulder, he hurried downstairs and out through the lodge's front door to where he'd parked his truck.

Stone, Kyla and Amanda stood beside the black Ford F-250, the one item he'd splurged on when he'd arrived in Montana. When he'd gone to work for Stone in Afghanistan, he'd sold his old truck.

Having nowhere to spend the money he'd earned, Carter had a sizeable amount saved. He'd considered purchasing a small ranch where he could raise a few cows and horses. That would give him purpose. At least he'd have livestock to come home to.

He tossed his duffel bag on the backseat and turned to face the three waiting beside the truck.

Amanda didn't look thrilled to ride with him back to the reservation. "I really should drive my car back."

"We'll bring it first thing in the morning," Stone assured her. "You two really need time to discuss your concerns and your cover story. The two-hour drive in the same vehicle will give you that."

Kyla touched Amanda's arm. "If you need anything, don't hesitate to call. Even if it's just to talk."

Amanda gave Kyla a crooked smile. "Sometimes, all I need is to vent. But not now. We need action. I don't want another teen to die. My job is to counsel them, give them guidance, help them navigate raging hormones, bullying and the temptation of drugs. If they're committing suicide, I feel personally responsible. I've failed them."

"You didn't force them to jump," Kyla reminded her.

"No, but I didn't give them the help they needed to avoid feeling like suicide was the only answer. The sooner we get back, the sooner we can find answers." Amanda glanced from Kyla to Stone and, finally, to Carter. "I'm ready."

He gave a curt nod and rounded the front of the truck to open the door for Amanda.

She gave him a slight smile and then climbed up into the cab and secured her seatbelt.

Carter closed the door and hurried around to the driver's side.

"Remember to use the resources we have available to us. Swede is amazing at ferreting out information from databases."

"Could you have him do a search on the Wind River Reservation, Bureau of Indian Affairs, DEA and the FBI?" Carter asked. "If those kids are playing in meth, there has to be a source, and all of those agencies should be aware of the problem and might have some insight into the operation."

"Will do," Stone grinned. "Enjoy getting to know your fiancée."

"Wait. That reminds me," Kyla said. "I have something you might need. Give me a minute. I'll be right back."

She dashed into the lodge.

Stone's gaze followed her. "I wonder what she forgot."

"No telling."

Two minutes later, Kyla burst through the lodge entrance and came to a stop in front of Carter. "You'll need this to make your engagement look more legit." She grabbed his hand and shoved a tissue into his open palm. Inside the tissue lay a delicate white-gold band with a clear, small, sparkling, marquis-cut diamond. "I found this at a pawn shop recently. It was so pretty, I couldn't resist."

Carter tried to give it back to Kyla. "No way. It looks expensive."

"I'd be afraid I'd lose it." Amanda shook her head. "We can't take it."

"Please," Kyla said. "I don't need it." She held up her hand to display a gorgeous solitaire ring on her left ring finger. I'm a little more attached to this one."

Stone slipped an arm around her. "And I'm a little more attached to this woman."

"You need the engagement to look real. The first thing a woman will ask is to see the ring," Kyla said.

Another vehicle pulled up in front of the lodge, and Chelsea, Benjamin Yates' woman, jumped out. "Oh, good. You've all met."

Benjamin came out of the lodge at that moment. "Hey, beautiful." He descended the steps from the porch and pulled Chelsea into his arms. "How's my favorite wolfologist?"

"Ah, you're back." She leaned up and kissed him full on the lips.

"Finished up this morning and got back here as soon as I could."

She slipped her arm around his waist and looked toward Amanda. "I take it you've assigned someone to help my friend Amanda?"

Benjamin lifted his chin toward Carter. "Carter's got this one."

"We were just working out the details of their engagement," Kyla added with a grin.

Chelsea's brow furrowed. "Engagement? Did I miss something?"

Stone chuckled. "Carter's going to the rez as her fiancé to avoid questions and the chance he'll be asked to leave."

"He just needs to put a ring on her finger and make it look real." Kyla nodded toward the ring in Carter's hand. "Go on. Make it legit."

After all the years he'd sworn he'd never take another wife, memories of that day his commanding officer had informed him of his wife's death rushed into his mind and threatened to over-whelm him.

He fought for control. "This is only an act. It isn't real."

"Right," Amanda said.

Carter hadn't realized he'd spoken his words aloud. "Sorry. I just want to be clear."

She nodded. "You'll be my fake fiancé, nothing more until we figure out what's going on. Besides, we barely know each other."

"Exactly." He held out the ring, expecting her to take it and slip it onto her finger.

"Wait," Kyla said. "I know this is all for show, but I feel like you should at least go through the motions of what it would be like if it were real. It would make the lies easier to tell."

His heart pounding hard against his ribs, Carter frowned. "That's ridiculous."

Kyla shook her head. "It will make it easier for Amanda to remember when people ask her how you proposed." She propped her fists on her hips. "Just do it and make it memorable."

Amanda's frown matched Carter's. "You don't have to. Just give me the ring."

The fact she was just as unwilling to stage the engagement as he was made it easier for Carter to "do it right."

Instead of handing her the ring, he dropped to one knee and looked up into her startlingly blue eyes. "Amanda, the fake love of my life, will you accept this ring as a symbol of our undying fake love and agree to marry me, which we both agree will never happen, and stay with me until death do us part or we resolve the suicide/murder case, whichever comes first?"

She laughed, her blue eyes dancing.

This was the first time he'd heard her laugh. The happy sound and the light in her eyes hit him square in his chest and cut a chink into the wall he'd carefully constructed around his heart.

For a moment, he couldn't breathe and couldn't see past the beauty of Amanda's happiness shining on her face.

She held out her hand. "In the name of getting

this show on the road, yes. I agree to this fake engagement, to pretend to love you and to act like we are prepared to spend the rest of our lives in wedded bliss."

Carter stood, slipped the ring on her finger and bent to press a kiss to her lips. "For show," he whispered.

"For show," she said in a hushed tone only he could hear.

"There," Kyla said. "Now, you're officially engaged."

"Fake engaged," Amanda corrected.

"Honey," Chelsea said, "you'll have to stop saying fake, or it will slip out while you're talking to the locals."

Carter wanted to argue that it was fake but knew she was right. "We'll work on that."

Amanda nodded. "Right now, we need to get going. I'd like to be back before dark and available should any of the teens need to talk to me."

Chelsea hugged Amanda. "You let me know if you need anything. And don't be such a stranger. We're all busy, but we need to make time for the people we care about."

Amanda's cheeks pinkened. "We do." She gave Chelsea a shaky smile. "Thank you for understanding."

"Don't thank me," Chelsea said. "Thank the Brotherhood Protectors. They'll make sure you stay safe."

Amanda's gaze met Carter's, her eyes narrowing a bit.

Did she think he couldn't keep her safe? He met her gaze and held it until she dropped hers. Yeah, she might not like the idea of him being with her all the time, but that was the only way he could keep her safe, twenty-four-seven.

He opened the passenger door and waited for her to climb in.

Once she was settled in her seat, he closed the door and rounded to the driver's side.

Stone waited for him there. "We're here if you need us. By us, I mean all of the Brotherhood Protectors here in West Yellowstone and in Eagle Rock. We can even tap on the Colorado division if needed."

Carter nodded. "Hopefully, we won't need to tap on anyone."

"Good luck." Stone stepped back as Carter slipped behind the steering wheel and started the truck.

The engine roared to life, and Carter backed out, turned and drove away from the lodge. He felt like he had whenever he'd deployed, only different.

On deployments, he'd had his team with him.

He shot a glance toward Amanda. He didn't know her, nor could he count on her to have his back. They hadn't trained together or been through anything life-threatening to learn each other's strengths and weaknesses. This would be a very different kind of assignment. He hoped he was up to flying mostly solo. He hoped he'd be enough.

First, he needed to know exactly what he was up against. Who was the enemy, what did they want and who stood in the way of them getting it? "Okay, start talking," he said abruptly. "I need to know what I'm getting into. If we take suicide off the table, who would want these particular teens dead? What's their motivation? What do you know about the teens? We need to know our enemy."

She shook her head. "The teens aren't the enemy," she said.

"I didn't say they were. Something they're doing, or are involved in, might be triggering a killer. All the more reason to understand the teens he's killing."

"I get that," Amanda said. "I've been trying to piece it together. So far, the three teens all belong to one group."

Carter shot a glance in Amanda's direction. "A gang?"

She nodded. "They call themselves the Young Wolves."

"Into drugs? Doing or selling?" he asked.

"That's just it. Until their deaths, I would've bet they weren't doing drugs. I never saw any of them high or heard of any showing up at school stoned."

"They could be good at hiding it."

She nodded. "One of the gang's members has been coming to me for grief counseling since the first suicide. It really got bad for her with the last one." Amanda sighed. "It was her twin brother. He jumped off a cliff. The M.E. said the first two had methamphetamines in their systems."

"That would be enough to push them over any edge," Carter said.

Amanda nodded. "Tara, my teen who's been coming to me, swore they never did drugs. They'd made a pact among themselves to stay clean. She did say that didn't always include the use of alcohol, but drugs were strictly avoided. She couldn't understand why her friends would've broken the gang's rules and messed with meth."

"Could someone from outside the gang be influencing them?" Carter asked.

"Maybe. There are other gangs bent on being the worst kind of people, acting out against any authority, be it tribal police or Wyoming State Police. Unemployment is high, which means they have too much time on their hands."

Carter nodded. "Time for them to get into trouble. What about gang warfare? Any other gangs pushing limits?"

"There is the Native American Syndicate, comprised of high school dropouts up to sixty-year-old motorcycle riders."

"Would they have reason to terrorize the Young Wolves?" Carter asked.

Amanda snorted. "They don't need a reason to do

anything. They terrorize for fun, and they're pretty blatant about it. Which doesn't make sense for them to kill and cover it up as suicides."

Carter spent a few moments digesting what Amanda had said thus far. After several minutes, he asked, "Who is the leader of the Young Wolves?"

"Keme Hunting Horse. He's nineteen, failed out of high school and won't go back to finish."

"GED?"

She shook her head. "I've tried to corner him a time or two, but he steers clear. He's Tara's boyfriend."

"We need to talk to him," Carter said.

"Good luck. Maybe you'll have a better shot at it, being male. He wasn't interested in talking with a counselor, but he might be interested in talking to just a man. His father served in the US Marine Corps and was killed early in the Iraqi war, leaving him without a father when he was eight."

"How do you know all that if he won't talk to you?"

"I have sources who've been on this reservation for a long time. They helped me fill in the blanks."

For the most part, the road was straight and didn't require a lot of Carter's attention to keep his truck between the ditches. "Did Tara say anything about the other victims?"

"She did," Amanda said. "Allison Sitting Dog was

first. She jumped off the bridge over the Little Wind River."

Carter looked toward Amanda. "And no one saw her?"

Amanda shook her head. "It was around one o'clock in the morning on a weekend. She'd told her mother she was going to stay the night at another girl's house.

"When she didn't come home the next morning, her mother called the other girl's home. That girl's mother didn't know anything about the girls planning a sleepover. Allison didn't sleep there, and her friend didn't know anything about a sleepover.

"A local guide leading a fishing trip on the Little Wind River found Allison's body on the rocks below the bridge. She was taken to the medical examiner. That's when they identified meth in her blood."

Carter cocked an eyebrow. "And she was a member of the gang that didn't do drugs?"

Amanda shrugged. "I'm just telling you what Tara told me."

"You said there were three suicides. Allison, Tara's brother and who else?"

"Ryan Gray Feather." Amanda looked out the front window. "Only sixteen years old. Just got his driver's license a couple of months back and was working part-time at a hamburger place in Riverton."

Carter shook his head. "So young."

"Tell me about it." Amanda's lips pressed into a thin line. "They had their whole lives in front of them. Why would they end it? From what Tara said, Ryan was working to put food on the table at home. His mother had skipped out on them, and his father couldn't work. He'd lost his foot due to complications with diabetes. Why would Ryan check out, knowing his family would be in worse shape without him?"

"That's a big burden on a kid, knowing he's the sole breadwinner," Carter pointed out.

"I know. Still, Tara said, he'd been doing well and managing the job, helping at home and getting passing grades in school. He was hoping to go to college so he could help even more."

"Who else is in this Young Wolves group?"

"Tara, Keme, the leader, KC Sun Dancer, a friend of Tara's, Dylan Many Paths, Josh Tall Grass, Nina Sweetwater and a few more I can't remember right off the top of my head."

"All of whom can be targeted next if the trend continues," Carter noted.

Amanda nodded. "I can't let another teen die. Something has to give so we can figure this out before another life is lost."

"Do you know anything about their group of friends?"

She shook her head. "I asked Tara what their common interests were and why they'd formed the group in the first place. All she said was that they were friends." Amanda's brow wrinkled. "She kind of cut me off and changed the subject."

"Like she wasn't telling you the whole truth?" Carter looked her way.

Amanda met his gaze briefly. "Yes. I feel like they're up to something she didn't want to talk about."

"If she doesn't want to lose another friend, she'll need to open up about what they're doing."

"Agreed. If not her, maybe I could talk to one of the others."

"Or I can," Carter said.

Amanda nodded. "Some of the guys might be more willing to talk to a man than a female counselor."

"So, what do we know?" Carter asked.

"The three teens were all part of the Young Wolves," Amanda said. "They aren't known for doing drugs. Many of them are helping out at home because either their parents can't work or they're not making enough money to keep food on the table."

"There is another gang with a seriously bad reputation on the rez. Perhaps some gang warfare going on?"

"That's something we can check into," Amanda agreed.

They talked more about the kids, life for them on the reservation and the challenges of poverty, unemployment and the casinos.

"Are they involved with anyone at the casino?" Carter asked.

"It's never come up in a conversation with Tara."

"Which doesn't mean they aren't involved, just that we need to cover that angle as well."

An hour had already passed, and they only had another hour to go before they arrived in Fort Washakie.

Amanda seemed no more excited to talk about their fake engagement than he did. But it had to be done.

He was about to say something when Amanda turned to him and blurted, "We should talk about—"

"—our engagement," he finished for her.

She sighed. "I was going to say our living arrangement, but yes, we need to come up with a story and commit it to memory."

"I find the best way to remember a lie is to make it as close to the truth as possible," he said.

Amanda stared across at him. "Do you lie often? I don't, and it makes me uncomfortable."

"No. I don't lie often. But going undercover means living a lie to keep you or the people you're working with safe."

She nodded. "I get that."

"If it makes you that uncomfortable to lie, I could stay in a hotel in Riverton, but you'd have to stay with me so I can keep an eye on you twenty-four-seven."

"And if I'm not available to the teens, they won't go out of their way to see me or trust me with their troubles. I need to be in Fort Washakie." She drew in a deep breath and let it out slowly. "Okay, how did we meet?"

He grinned. "We nearly had a head-on collision. My horse, your car."

Amanda's lips twisted. "Truth." Her eyebrows dipped. "Why were you riding that horse so fast around a blind curve?"

"It wasn't my choice. He's called Diablo for a reason. I was just doing my part to train him not to go bat-shit crazy when he's let out of the barnyard."

Amanda chuckled. "Who was training who?"

"Diablo won that match, but I haven't given up."

"Where was our first date?" she asked.

"At the Grand Yellowstone Lodge," Carter answered.

"And we already know how you proposed," Amanda said, staring down at the ring on her left hand. "It's a beautiful ring. I still feel nervous wearing it."

He reached across and took her hand in his, squeezing it gently. "It'll be okay," he said, though he wasn't so sure about the jolt of electricity that just blasted through him at the simple touch. He let go of her hand and replaced his on the steering wheel.

Holy hell. What was that?

She drew her hand into her lap and covered it with her other one.

"We don't know anything about each other," she said. "Shouldn't an engaged couple know each other's life history?"

He nodded. "I was born and raised in Texas in a small town where we joined the FFA and rode horses for fun. Did a little bronc riding as a teen until I got smart and joined the Navy."

"A military man," she said.

"I worked hard to become a Navy SEAL and spent a lot of tours in the Middle East, fighting the Taliban and ISIS among other more exotic locations."

Amanda shot a glance his way. "I didn't even think about it, but are you married? If so, I don't think I can pretend to be engaged to you, knowing you have a wife and children somewhere."

His chest tightened, and his hands squeezed the steering wheel. "I was."

"Will I be a fake stepmother to your children?" Amanda asked softly.

"No," Carter said.

"I'm sorry," Amanda said. "Did your ex get full custody?"

He shook his head. "There is no ex and no children."

Amanda frowned. "But you were married—" Her eyes rounded. "Oh, I'm so sorry. How? If you don't mind my asking. Just tell me to shut up if you do."

"It's okay. It happened over five years ago." He hadn't talked to anyone about that part of his life other than during the required mental health check with a specialist he'd been forced to see to prove he was still competent to fight as a Navy SEAL. Something about Amanda, maybe the way she spoke so softly or the way she cared about the kids on the reservation, made him want to open up to her. "She was murdered in her bed by a burglar."

"Oh, sweet Jesus." Amanda pressed her fingers to her lips. "And were you injured?"

He shook his head, his lip pulling back in a self-deprecating sneer. "I was safe on the other side of the world, fighting a war we would never win, while she lay in her bed, pregnant with our baby girl."

"That's awful," Amanda said. "But you can't blame yourself."

"The hell I can't. I should've been there for them."

Amanda shook her head. "You had a job to do."

"I could've left the military and found work as a civilian where I was home at night to defend my family."

"You couldn't have known that would happen. You could've been on a sales trip with your civilian job or working a night shift in a factory."

"Or I could've been home when that guy broke in."

"And he could've killed you along with your wife," Amanda pointed out.

He slammed his palm against the steering wheel. "Then I wouldn't have known what it was like to have my heart ripped out of my chest, or what it was like to want to end my life because I didn't deserve to be alive while she was dead."

Amanda reached out to touch his arm. "Are you going to be okay with this fake engagement? We don't have to do it, you know. You can just be a friend coming to visit for a couple of weeks. I'm sure that will work just as well."

He shook his head. "No. I'm okay. Really. I promise not to let my past interfere with our investigation. It's been five years. I should be over it."

"Seems to me you never let yourself be over it. You feel like you let her down and deserve to suffer because of it."

"Thanks for trying," he said, "but save your counseling for the teens. I've seen my share of shrinks. I'm doing fine. I'm not addicted to drugs or alcohol, and I can hold a job. What more do I need?"

"To move on with your life. To quit beating yourself up for something you had no control over."

"Again, save your counseling for the kids. They're the ones who are committing suicide. Not me."

She nodded. "Fair enough."

A long silence stretched between them. Finally, he said, "You know my story…what's yours?"

She gave him a crooked grin. "Not nearly as illustrious as yours. I wasn't fighting the Taliban or saving lives in a war zone. I spent my first eleven years living in a shitty trailer on the Wind River Reservation, where my father beat my mother and me whenever he felt like it. I ended up in the foster system at the age of eleven and lost count of the number of homes I was moved around to between eleven and sixteen."

"Your parents?"

"Mom got tired of my dad beating her and me. She dropped me at the police station in Casper and disappeared. When the police tried to send me home to dear old Dad, he refused to take responsibility for me. I stayed in the foster system until I was sixteen, and Joe Sharp Spear rescued me and took me back to the reservation."

"To your dad?"

"Hell no," she said. "I stayed with Joe. He taught me that I could be better than what I'd come from. I finished high school and went on to college, where I worked to get my undergraduate degree in psychology and a master's in counseling. I wanted to help kids like me to believe in themselves like Joe taught me." She smiled. "Joe saved me."

"And you want on to pay it forward by saving the teens you're working with?" he guessed.

She nodded. "They deserve better. They just have to believe in themselves."

"And have a safe environment in which to grow

and thrive." He nodded. "I'll do my best to help you make that happen."

"Thank you." She snorted softly. "Like you, I feel like I've failed the ones who are already gone. I should've been there for them."

He frowned in her direction. "You couldn't have known they were going to die."

She met his gaze. "And you couldn't have known your wife would die. We can't be everywhere. We can only do the best we can when and where we are at the time."

What Amanda was saying was much like what the other mental health specialists had said. Only he hadn't been ready to listen and accept that what they'd said was true. Maybe it was the five years past that made him more willing to come to terms with Tracey's death. Or maybe it was Amanda.

Either way, he needed to help this woman, and in so doing, make up for not being there for Tracey.

CHAPTER 5

AMANDA SPENT the last twenty minutes of the trip in silence, going over everything they'd discussed, coming back to the fact Carter was a widower who'd lost his wife and child to murder. And here he was helping her determine whether they were dealing with a serial killer targeting the teens on the Wind River Reservation.

She couldn't decide if this mission was a mistake for him or a chance at atonement.

As they closed in on the tiny town of Fort Washakie, she realized they had to set aside their tragic pasts and focus on what mattered—helping the kids.

With an hour of daylight still clinging to the sky, Amanda could show Carter around and familiarize him with the buildings and facilities in the town where tribal headquarters resided for the Eastern

Shoshoni and the Norther Arapahoe tribes who shared the Wind River Reservation. As small as the town was, it wouldn't take five minutes to point out anything of interest.

"I'd like to stop at my office and check my messages," Amanda said.

Carter nodded. "Just tell me which way to turn."

"Right here," she said.

Two turns within a couple of blocks placed them in front of a small building that had been a house at one time and had been converted into a mental health clinic, where people could come in without running the gauntlet of other healthcare professionals and patients.

Carter shifted into park and killed the engine.

Amanda shoved open her door and dropped to the ground. She fished in her purse for the keys to the building. Once she found them, she unlocked the door and stepped inside, flipping on the light switch. Everything was like she'd left it when she'd made the mad dash to West Yellowstone, looking for help.

The light on her old-fashioned answering machine blinked two times, meaning she had two messages. Amanda pressed the button.

The first was a salesperson offering her the deal of a lifetime on siding for her home. "I don't own a home," she muttered.

"Did you say something?" Carter said from across the room as he stood beside the entrance.

"Nothing worth repeating," she answered back.

A young woman's voice played on the next message. "Ms. Small, this is Tara. If you're there, we need your help. Please come to my home when you get this message. I would come to you, but I have my little brother and sister tonight. Mom's working at the casino."

"Have you given them your cell phone number?" Carter asked.

"No. But I will. I need them to know I'll do whatever it takes to help."

Carter led the way to the door and opened it for Amanda. "Are we going straight there?"

"Yes." She would've liked to talk with the tribal police chief for an update on anything happening since Tobi Running Fox's leap off the cliff. At the very least, Amanda wanted to know if the labs had come back. Had Tobi been high on meth when he'd leaped from the cliff?

However, Tara's cry for help came first.

Carter stepped out of the building and held the door for Amanda. Once outside, she turned and locked the door.

"I'm surprised Tara's mother is working tonight," Carter said. "Seems too soon after the death of her son."

Amanda hurried toward Carter's truck. "She doesn't have much of a choice. If she misses a day of work, someone else will gladly take her job. She's lucky she has one. The casinos employ the members of the tribe, but there aren't enough jobs to employ all of them. Tara's mother can't afford to quit or be replaced. She has four…three children at home to feed and clothe."

She didn't wait for Carter to get to the passenger door first. Instead, she opened her own door and climbed up inside the cab.

Carter wisely went straight for the driver's seat. As soon as they were all in and buckled, he backed out of the parking space and pulled out onto the road. "Which way?"

"Turn right. The Running Fox family lives in a mobile home park on the south side of town. The road in and out is gravel and turns to muck and slush in the winter. I visited Tara and Tobi shortly after the first suicide. It was at their mother's request. Allison Sitting Dog was a friend Tara and Tobi grew up with. They took it pretty hard. I remember Tara staring at her hands, shaking her head, saying, 'This shouldn't have happened.'"

"Did she say anything about Allison's state of mind? Could she think of any reason Allison would've been so depressed that she would commit suicide?"

Amanda shook her head. "Tara said Allison was fine when she'd talked to her earlier that day. She was distraught at losing her friend. When Tobi died…" She frowned. "Tara was hysterical."

Carter slowed as he approached a curve in the road. "Understandable, considering it was her brother."

Amanda clutched her hands together. "I hope Tara's all right. She sounded…I don't know…"

"A little desperate?" Carter suggested.

"Yes," Amanda said. "I hope she's not considering suicide like the others. If that's what this is all about."

"There has to be something else going on that she hasn't told you," Carter said.

"And maybe she's ready to tell me." Amanda's lips pressed into a tight line. "I hope that's the case. I don't want another teen to die."

"I'm betting Tara doesn't want any more of her friends to die as well." Carter reached over and touched her arm. "We'll figure this out."

"Damn right, we will." Amanda's nerves tingled where his fingers brushed against her skin. She had to force herself to focus on the road ahead when she wanted to turn toward the man driving. "Turn right at the entrance to the mobile home park. The Running Fox's trailer is in the back corner. Tara won't be expecting anyone to be with me. Let me approach her first."

Carter drove to the back of the lot where a single-wide mobile home stood with rickety wooden steps leading up to the front door. What little skirting that had been wrapped around the bottom of the trailer hung loose in several spots, bent and jagged where the wind had ripped it away.

As Carter shifted into park, the front door opened, and a dark-haired teen stepped out. Two younger children crowded around her legs, their dark eyes rounding as Carter climbed down from his truck.

Amanda was already on the ground and hurrying around the front of the truck by the time Carter closed his door.

"Tara," Amanda said from the bottom of the steps. "I came as soon as I got back in town."

Tara's eyes narrowed as she stared at Carter. "Who's he?"

Amanda forced a smile to her face and turned toward Carter. "Tara, this is my...fiancé, Carter. Carter, this is my friend, Tara."

Tara's frown deepened. "You never said you were engaged."

"I wasn't until today." Amanda hated lying to the teen. But she needed the girl to accept Carter's presence. "He surprised me with a ring when I visited my friend in West Yellowstone." She held up her left hand. "See? Isn't it beautiful?"

The boy on Tara's left leaned close and whispered in Tara's ear.

She looked down at him. "It's okay. Ms. Small is a friend, not a stranger."

The boy pointed to Carter. "What about him?"

Tara met Amanda's gaze.

"It's okay, Tara. Carter is one of the good guys. I wouldn't be engaged to him if he wasn't. He drove me here because my car is in the shop back in West Yellowstone. I have someone bringing it to me tomorrow when they're done fixing it."

Tara stared hard at Amanda and Carter for a long moment before finally turning to the kids at her sides. "Go get into your pajamas. It's time for bed."

The little girl hugged Tara's leg. "Do we have to?"

Tara stroked the dark hair on the child's head. "Yes, Tina, you do."

"Tobi used to carry me to my bed," the girl said, her eyes welling with tears.

"I can carry you," Tara said, her eyes filling. "And Tommy will read to you."

"I want Tobi," Tina cried.

"I do, too," Tara said, "but he's not here."

"When is he coming home?" Tina sobbed, burying her face in Tara's belly.

Tara knelt beside the little girl and pulled her into his arms. "He's not coming home. So, we have to figure out how to do things without him." She held onto the child as she straightened, lifting her.

Tina wrapped her arms around Tara's neck, her legs around her waist and leaned her cheek against her sister's neck and sniffled. "I miss Tobi."

"I know," Tara said. "We all do." She looked over

the child's shoulder at Amanda and Carter. "I'll be back after I get Tina and Tommy into their beds."

"Can I help?" Amanda asked.

Tara shook her head. "I can handle this. Please, wait out here."

Amanda nodded. "Take your time. They need you."

Tara gave her a hint of a smile.

Tommy opened the door for her, and the teen entered, carrying her younger sister.

After the door closed behind her, Amanda turned toward Carter. "Thank you for being here with me."

He nodded, his gaze on the door to the trailer. "I wish I could do more."

"Me, too." Amanda worried about the burden Tara shouldered. When her twin had been alive, they'd shared the burden of caring for the two younger kids. Now, it was all on Tara.

Carter closed the distance between them and slipped an arm around her.

Amanda jumped when his hand came to rest on the small of her back.

He bent to whisper in her ear, "She seemed to be hesitant even when you said I was your fiancé. We need to make it appear more real."

"Yes," Amanda said, her voice breathy in response to every place his body touched hers. "We do." Despite her need to act like a newly engaged woman, Amanda held her body stiffly, afraid Carter would realize just what an effect he was having on her.

The engagement was all a show to keep him undercover as her fake fiancé. She shouldn't be so hyper-aware of the Navy SEAL's incredibly appealing body.

It was important for the teens and the tribal elders to accept this man and trust him, as Amanda would trust someone she'd promised to marry.

What seemed like hours later, though in fact had only been a few minutes, Tara appeared on the small porch, carrying an envelope in her hands. She shot a glance over her shoulder, back into their home. "I think they're down for the night, but I'd rather we talk out here." She descended the steps, her gaze on Carter.

Amanda touched the girl's arm. "I can vouch for Carter. I told him about what happened with Allison, Ryan and now…Tobi."

Carter nodded. "I'm sorry for your loss. Nothing is easy about losing someone you love." He met the girl's gaze with a compelling one of his own. "I know how it feels."

Tara's eyes welled, and tears slipped down her cheeks. "I found this tucked into my diary this afternoon when I came home from school." She shoved the envelope into Amanda's hands and then sat on the steps, burying her face in her hands.

Amanda opened the envelope and pulled out a

sheet of notebook paper with jerky handwriting filling the page.

Though the sun had dipped below the horizon, the sky had just enough gray light left for Amanda to read the words.

Tara,

If you're reading this, something has happened to me. But I wanted you to know I would never commit suicide and leave you and Mom to take care of Tommy and Tina on your own.

I don't believe Allison or Ryan took their own lives. They were looking forward to getting out of the mess the Young Wolves got themselves into just as much as the rest of us.

I'm afraid more of us will suffer if we don't get help. I didn't speak with Keme about what I was going to do or even you because I don't know who might be listening. It appears as though someone knows too much. Someone who doesn't have the best interests of the Wolves at heart and is using what we've discussed in private to target us.

If you're reading this letter, they got to me before I could get to the authorities and tell them what we discussed the last time we all met—before Ryan and Allison.

I'm sorry I let you down. Please tell Mom I'm sorry for what I got you into and for not being there to help. Tell her I love her and none of this is her fault. It's all on me.

I love you, Tara. Give Tommy and Tina a hug from their big brother and tell them how much I love them, too.

Until we meet again in the spirit world.

Tobi

A lump lodged in Amanda's throat as she read the words the teen had scratched on the paper. When she finished, she handed the letter to Carter and turned to Tobi's silently sobbing twin.

"Oh, Tara," Amanda sat on the step beside the girl and wrapped her arm around her. "I'm so sorry. Tobi was a good young man who cared about you and your family."

"He would do anything for us," Tara said, her voice catching on another sob. "That's why he agreed to do what we were doing."

"What was it you were doing?" Amanda said.

Tara buried her face in her palms. "I can't."

"Can't what?"

"Can't tell you," the teen said through her hands. "Only the Young Wolves can know. We were sworn to secrecy."

"How can I help you if I don't know the whole story?" Amanda asked.

"I can't."

"Don't you think it's worth breaking your word if it keeps you from losing another member of your group?" Amanda asked.

Tara's sobs slowed and finally stopped. When she looked up, she stared through watery eyes into Amanda's gaze. "We were going to get out. It was our plan. One last time and we were going to stop."

"One more time doing what?" Amanda persisted.

Tara shook her head. "I can't."

Amanda wanted to shake the girl. "Lives could depend on you telling me what you know, Tara."

The teen lifted her chin. "Lives depend on me keeping the secret." She looked past Amanda to the mobile homes around them and the shadows deepening as the little bit of light faded from the sky. "I've already said too much."

"And not nearly enough." Amanda sighed. "I'm not giving up on you." She pulled a business card out of her back pocket and handed it to Tara. "I wrote my personal cell phone number on the back of that card. If you need me, you can call me any time, day or night."

Tara took the card and stared down at the number written on the back. "Thank you."

Carter held up the letter. "Do you mind if I take a picture of the letter?"

Tara frowned. "Why?"

"I know Amanda will want to study this to analyze what Tobi was feeling at the time he wrote this. It might help her to help you and the rest of the Young Wolves."

Tara shrugged. "Whatever. I don't think that letter will help you do anything. I just wanted you to know Tobi didn't commit suicide. He wouldn't willingly have left us to make it on our own."

"Tobi was a good brother to you," Amanda said.

"Yes, he was," Tara said. "The best. I just wish he'd

confided in me. Who was he going to meet? He might have thought he was going to the right person, and that person turned out to be the one preying on us. I could've been his backup, and he might not have ended up at the bottom of that cliff." She inhaled a shaky breath.

"Tara, we need to know as much as possible about the Young Wolves. Were you involved in something that might make you targets of another gang?"

Tara shook her head and backed toward the mobile home's door. "I can't say anything else. Tobi didn't commit suicide, and he didn't do drugs. I don't care what the labs say. If he had drugs in his system, he didn't put them there by himself. Same as Allison and Ryan. We made a pact when we formed the Young Wolves. We wouldn't take the drugs."

She opened the trailer door and stepped inside. "You've already been here too long. Please, leave." She looked past them as if searching for someone else watching them. Then she closed the door.

Amanda wanted to follow Tara inside and make her tell her everything she was holding back.

Carter took Amanda's hand, drew it through the crook of his arm and walked her back to his truck.

When they reached the passenger side, Amanda turned back. "Do you think—"

He squeezed her hand on his arm and whispered, "We'll talk later."

As Amanda climbed into the truck, her gaze

remained on the mobile home containing a teen and two young children. Her chest tightened.

"They were a team, Tobi and Tara. Twins who worked to help their mother provide for the family." She gave one last glance at the mobile home at the back of the trailer park, then focused on the shadows, much as Tara had done. As far as she could tell, no one lurked in the shadows.

Once they were out of the small trailer park and back on the road, Carter shot her a brief look. "Did you pick up on what Tara said about the drugs?"

Amanda frowned. "That they don't do drugs?"

Carter shook his head. "That's not how she put it. She said they made a pact. They don't take *the* drugs."

"That's what I said," Amanda turned to Carter.

"When you talk to people, they'll tell you they don't 'do' drugs. Tara said they take the drugs."

"I don't see the difference."

"And maybe there isn't a difference." Carter focused on the road leading back into Fort Washakie. "But it was almost like they don't take the drugs that are available to them. Like they have them, but they don't take them."

"Why would they have drugs and not take them?" As soon as Amanda said the words, she realized the answer. "Do you think they're dealing drugs?"

Carter shrugged. "I don't know. What I do know is that Tara was spooked. The Young Wolves have secrets they're willing to die for."

"Willing or not, they're dying." Amanda's lips pressed together. "If Tara won't talk, we'll take this discussion to Tara's boyfriend, Keme Hunting Horse."

"The leader of the Young Wolves," Carter said. "Do you know where we can find him?"

Amanda shook her head. "No, but I know someone who does. The Chief of Tribal Police."

Carter's brow wrinkled. "If the teens fear someone, they're not going to want the police involved."

Amanda nodded. "Chief Sharp Spear knows everyone on the reservation and where they live. It's the quickest way to locate Keme."

"Sharp Spear? Any relation to Joe Sharp Spear, your foster dad?"

She gave him a crooked smile. "One and the same. I had no choice but to march the straight and narrow with Joe looking over my shoulder the whole way."

"You're still close to him?"

She nodded, a smile curving her lips. "I love him like the dad I should've had instead of the one I got." Her brow furrowed. "The question is, do we tell him our engagement is fake? I don't like lying to the man. He deserves better from me."

"I'm sure he'll understand when this case is solved. The only people on this reservation who should know I'm not who I say I am are you and me. The more people who know, the more likely it will get out to everyone else."

Amanda nodded. "I hope you're right and that Joe

will understand. He's a good man who cares about his people. And he has a firm grasp on what he considers right and wrong."

"If we want him to believe we're engaged," Carter shot a glance her way, "we'll have to put on a good show of being a couple in love."

Amanda held his gaze for the brief moment he held hers. Not until he turned his attention back to the road ahead did she take another breath.

This fake engagement was more complicated than she'd thought it would be. Especially since she was finding herself highly attracted to the former Navy SEAL. How could she pretend to be in love while falling in love and trying not to let Carter know she was more and more drawn to him?

The man wasn't interested in a relationship. He'd been in love with the wife he'd lost. She could never fill that empty place in his heart. And she wasn't sure she could settle for being a poor substitute.

She heaved a long sigh.

"Exhausted?" he asked.

Amanda snorted softly. "Just a little."

CHAPTER 6

CARTER FOLLOWED Amanda's directions to the tribal police station he'd passed on the way into Fort Washakie from West Yellowstone. A Wind River Police service vehicle stood out front.

"Hopefully, that's the chief's SUV," Amanda said.

As soon as Carter parked, Amanda shoved open her door and dropped to the ground. She met Carter in front of the truck and held out her hand. "Feeling engaged?" she asked with a wink and a smile.

"It's starting to sink in," he said with an answering smile. He couldn't help but smile when she looked at him that way. And why not? They were supposed to be a newly engaged couple, happily in love yet still concerned for the well-being of the teens on the reservation.

He took her hand in his and strode beside her through the entrance to the station.

A tall, dark-skinned man stood with his back to the door, a phone pressed to his ear. "Yes, Mrs. Light Feather, I know there's a horse in your garden. Officer Stockley is on his way out to your place now. He should be there in ten minutes." The man nodded. "I know a horse can destroy an entire row of corn in less than ten minutes. Officer Stockley will be there soon. He'll take care of it. No, I'm sorry, he won't replant your garden for you."

The chief pushed a hand through his dark hair and turned with a frown. "I have to go now, Mrs. Light Feather. That's right. Police business. Say hello to your son for me when he gets home from work. Yes, ma'am. Goodbye." He ended the call and laid the receiver in its cradle. When he straightened, his gaze went to where Carter held Amanda's right hand, and his frown deepened. "Amanda, who have you got with you?"

She shifted beside Carter, and a soft blush rose up her neck and filled her cheeks. "Hi, Joe, I thought you should be the first to know...I'm engaged," she blurted and held up her left hand, flashing the engagement ring Kyla had been right to loan her.

For a long moment, Joe stared at the ring on her hand and then into her eyes. When he didn't say anything, she pulled Carter forward. "Joe, this is Carter Manning, my fiancé. Carter, this is Joe Sharp Spear, my foster father." She smiled, albeit a tight one. "Please say something."

Carter held out his hand. "I'm sorry to spring this on you. I should've asked her father for her hand before asking her. But I was too excited and couldn't wait. Please, forgive me for jumping the gun."

Joe took Carter's hand, his eyes narrow as he gave him a firm, tending toward bone-crunching, handshake. "Carter Manning. I don't recall Amanda ever speaking of a Carter Manning. Ever. You'll have to excuse my reticence at her announcement. Do I need to do a background check on you? Or maybe a drug test on my daughter?"

Carter chuckled. "If it makes you feel better, sir, do both. My record is clean, and, as far as I can tell, Amanda hasn't done drugs the entire time I've known her."

"And how long is that?" Joe's head tipped backward, and he stared down his broad nose at Carter. "How long have you known Amanda?"

His smile straightened as he met Joe's challenging glare. "Long enough to know she's the woman I want to share the rest of my life with." He released Joe's hand and reclaimed Amanda's. "She's amazing, smart, caring and beautiful. I want nothing more than to be with her."

Joe's frown grew fiercer. "And does that mean you're taking her away from the reservation?"

Carter shook his head. "I'll go to wherever makes her happy. If that's here on the Wind River Reservation, then this is where I'll stay."

"How will you provide for her when the unemployment rate on the reservation is so high and crime is two and a half times greater than the national average?"

"I've been in tougher situations in places with worse unemployment and poverty. I have a job with a security firm. I can base out of anywhere."

"Joe," Amanda touched his arm. "Carter is a Navy SEAL."

Joe's eyes widened briefly. "You don't say?"

Carter nodded. "I left the Navy a few years ago and joined a private security firm protecting American workers in Afghanistan until the US pulled out."

"Honorable or dishonorable discharge from the Navy," Joe barked out.

Carter smiled briefly. "Honorable. I loved my work as a Navy SEAL, defending our country."

"Then why did you leave the service?" the police chief asked.

"Joe," Amanda said, "he had his reasons. This isn't an interrogation."

"The hell it isn't. I don't care if he was related to Mother Teresa and gave alms to the poor in some godforsaken third-world county. No man springs it on me that he's engaged to my girl without an explanation and a background check."

Amanda gave the police chief a lopsided grin. "You don't let much get past you, do you?" She leaned up and gave him a hug. "Can't you just be happy for me?"

He hugged her back, the frown creasing his forehead relaxing slightly. "I want you to be happy more than anything. I just don't know this man. Until I do, you two will have to suffer the third degree."

Carter nodded solemnly. "Understood. I'd feel the same if it were my daughter."

"So, you have a daughter?" Joe snapped.

That punch to the gut never got better. His child had never had the chance to grow up, much less be born. "No, sir."

If he'd been home to protect his wife, he might have had a daughter...and a wife. He wouldn't be there pretending to be engaged to Amanda. Though the more he pretended, the more it felt strangely...right.

"Married before?" Joe asked.

"Once," Carter admitted.

"Did she file or you?"

"Joe, enough." Amanda touched a hand to the big man's chest. "Carter is a widower, and you're making him uncomfortable."

"It's okay, Amanda," Carter said gently before he faced Joe. "I was married; my pregnant wife was murdered in her bed by a burglar." He lifted his chin. "I was deployed at the time."

Joe's frown eased. "I'm sorry." He looked from Carter to Amanda. "Does he make you happy?"

Amanda nodded. "Very."

"Then that's all that matters." Joe glared again at Carter. "Keep it that way, or you'll have to answer to me."

Carter stood at attention, just short of popping a salute. "Yes, sir."

"Navy SEAL, huh?" Joe's lips twitched on the corners. "Feel a little land-locked here?"

"Not at all, sir," Carter said. "Most of my deployments were on land. The only water I saw was during BUD/S and other training missions." He grinned. "I grew up in south-central Texas. Not much water there."

"Then how did you end up a Navy SEAL? That requires a significant amount of swimming."

Carter nodded. "My high school track coach challenged me to participate in an ironman triathlon. I had to learn to swim well enough to compete. When I wasn't riding broncs in the regional rodeos or hauling hay for the local ranchers, I was running, bicycling and swimming."

"Did you have time to be a kid?"

Carter chuckled. "Yes, sir. But not enough time to get into too much trouble."

Joe's lips turned downward. "That's the problem out here. The kids have too much unsupervised time on their hands. There aren't enough adults to rein them in or jobs to keep them employed."

Amanda nodded. "Which gives them too many

opportunities to get in trouble, be depressed or get lost in the vast distances on the reservation."

"We don't have enough law enforcement personnel to cover the 2.2 million acres. It's over three thousand square miles and fewer law enforcement personnel than they have in Washington, D.C.," Joe said. "It takes a special person to want to stay and try to make a difference." He nodded toward Amanda.

"What are you talking about? You're the one making the difference," Amanda said. "You've been working in law enforcement for how many years now?"

"It'll be thirty, come September." He met Carter's gaze. "Point is, we don't have nearly enough people who care to help."

Amanda grimaced. "What he's trying to say is don't take me away. I'm needed here."

Carter held up a hand. "I won't take her to go anywhere she doesn't want to go."

Joe nodded. "Good."

"We came to tell you of our engagement," Amanda said. "But we also need some help."

"With what?" Joe asked.

"I'm worried about the teens in the Young Wolves group after the three apparent suicides." Amanda lifted her chin and met Joe's gaze. "I'd like to meet with Keme Hunting Horse, their leader, to see if there's anything I can do to help."

Joe's frown returned. "You don't want to go out to the Hunting Horse place. It's not safe."

"I need to talk to Keme," Amanda insisted. "Besides, I'll have Carter with me."

Joe stared from Amanda to Carter and back. "Oscar Hunting Horse is a mean drunk. I've had to answer to a number of domestic disturbances at his place, all involving his beating up on his wife."

"Bastard," Amanda muttered.

"Watch your mouth, little lady," Joe said automatically.

Amanda's lips twisted in a wry grin. "You say worse."

"I do, but it doesn't make it right." He waved a hand. "It doesn't matter. You're a grown woman about to get married. You can curse all you want. Your fiancé can probably teach you a few new ones."

Carter gave Joe a crooked smile. "I'll try to restrain myself."

"As I was saying, Oscar is a mean drunk. Every time I went out there, one of the kids called. The wife refused to press charges. Oscar is the only one with a job. If she has him thrown in jail, they have no money to buy food and clothing for their five children, three of whom are under the age of seven."

"Even if she could find a job, she couldn't afford daycare for the three youngest," Amanda noted.

"Right," Joe said with a nod. "Keme is the oldest. He works part-time at the local tavern, washing dishes to help the family. His brother has been hanging out with a rival gang, trying to find his way down the wrong path, while his big brother is doing all the right things."

Amanda pressed her lips together. "Sounds like I need to talk to Keme's brother, too."

"Anything you can do to set them on the right path would be better than nothing," Joe said. "But really, you don't want to be out there when Oscar is home." Joe glanced at his watch. "He works alternating shifts at the Chemical company in Riverton. If you go out now, look for his burnt orange pickup. If it's not there, he's not there." He gave them the address and directions. "GPS doesn't always work on the rez. If you're going to talk to Keme, check the tavern first to see if he's working tonight."

Amanda leaned up and kissed Joe's cheek. "Thank you, Joe. You know I love you."

"Yeah. Until you went off and got yourself engaged." He shook his head. "I see where I rank."

"I have enough love in my heart for both of you," she said.

"Now, if you'll excuse me," Joe glanced at his watch. "I have to give Heather Smoke Signal a ride home from the tavern. It's about that time."

Joe led the way out of the station, climbed into his SUV and drove toward the south end of town and the Gray Wolf Tavern.

"What does he mean giving Heather a ride home?"

"Heather works as a janitor at the high school from five-thirty to three-thirty in the afternoon. She spends the next couple of hours at the tavern drinking. Joe gives her a ride home to keep her from a DUI or from wandering around, ripe for a public intoxication charge. She sleeps it off and is bright and cheerful the next morning for work."

Carter shook his head. "Joe's a saint."

"He cares about the people he serves and does his best to take care of them. So many residents of the reservation are bent on destroying their lives through alcohol, drugs or fighting."

"And now, potentially, suicide."

"Oh, we have our share of suicides," Amanda said.

"Then why do you think the latest aren't suicides —other than one of the members of the group telling you different?"

"We've had our share of suicides, just not so many, so close together and within the same group of friends." Amanda paused with her hand on the door handle to the passenger side of the truck. "It doesn't feel right. And Tara was scared like she was afraid she was being watched."

"Or like she might be next," Carter said.

"We can't let that happen. It's bad enough the other three are gone. We can't lose another child to murder or suicide."

"Let's find Keme and see if he will open up about what's going on." Carter rounded the front of the truck and slid behind the steering wheel. He turned the truck around and headed for the tavern a few blocks from the police station.

Carter left Amanda in the truck while he ran in to ask if Keme was working that night.

The manager said he wasn't working until the following night. Carter thanked him and hurried back out to the truck.

"Not working," he said as he climbed in, backed up the truck and headed out of town toward the Hunting Horse place, praying the man of the house was still at work.

Carter had no doubt he could handle whatever Oscar might throw his way. He didn't want Amanda, Keme or the rest of the Hunting Horse family traumatized should the head of the household blow a gasket because someone dared to step foot on their property.

He also didn't want Keme to take flak from his father because someone came to talk to the teen, not the father. The man sounded like he looked for reasons to be an asshole and get rough with the people he was supposed to love.

"I don't understand men who can be so brutal to their family members. I had a hard time accepting the macho mentality of the Middle East. It always burned me up that they treated their women worse than they treated their livestock." Carter shook his head.

"We'll just have to talk with Keme and leave before his father shows up. Or we turn around and leave if we see Oscar's truck there." Amanda touched Carter's arm. "You don't have to go in. I can talk with Keme by myself."

He looked at her. "The hell you will. His father hits women."

"I won't let him get close enough to hit me," Amanda said.

"You're not going in by yourself." Carter directed a heavy frown in her direction. "Period."

Amanda tilted her head. "You know, I got around this reservation just fine without you."

"Yeah, but I'm here now, and my job is to protect you and help you find out what's going on. I can't do that if I'm not with you." His jaw hardened, his hands gripping the steering wheel so tight his knuckles turned white. "I go where you go."

"Is there where I salute and say, *Sir, yes, sir*?" she quipped and grinned. "Did you know that you get a tick in the side of your face when you're stern and determined to get your way?"

Carter frowned. "You're changing the subject."

"No. I thought we had finished the discussion. Where I go, you go. Isn't that the conclusion you came to?" She cocked an eyebrow.

His continued to frown. "I get the feeling you're only humoring me."

"Trust me; I'm not finding anything about what's happening on this reservation humorous."

"You'll take me with you wherever you go?"

Amanda touched a finger to her chin. "Except the bathroom. I do draw the line on some things. A girl has to have some privacy." She pointed ahead. "Turn right at the next road."

He slowed and turned off the highway onto a gravel road. The roar of tires on loose gravel made it impossible to talk. And he wanted to say more. Amanda hadn't actually agreed to take him with her wherever she went. She'd made it sound like she had, but in reality, she hadn't.

"Slow down. We should see their house at the end of this driveway," Amanda said in a hushed voice. "Can you turn off your headlights?"

He found the switch and killed the headlights. About that time, they rounded a bend in the road and approached a house a hundred yards ahead with lights glowing in the windows.

Dusk had settled over the plains, making the darkened outbuildings blend with the shadows.

An old refrigerator leaned against a dilapidated shed. Worn tires lay in a stack under a tree beside what appeared to be a piece of antique farm equipment. The rusted body of an old 1940s truck stood on concrete blocks, missing all four wheels.

The house hadn't seen paint in years; the wooden siding was gray with weather and age. The porch across the front sagged on one corner, along with the roof.

"No orange truck," Amanda declared. "I hope Keme is home."

The front door opened, and a thin woman stepped out, rubbing her hands along the sides of her faded jeans. Her dark hair hung down her back with random streaks of gray.

Carter parked a couple of yards away from the front of the house and got out.

Amanda jumped down and met him at the front of the truck. "Mrs. Hunting Horse?"

The woman's eyes narrowed. "That's me. You're trespassing on our property. You need to leave." She looked past them as if expecting another vehicle to show up anytime.

"Ma'am, I'm Amanda Small, the tribal counselor. I was hoping to speak to Keme. We're worried about him after losing his friends. Is he home?"

A tall, thin young man with long, straight black hair stepped through the door behind the woman. He wore a black T-shirt with the faded image of a rock band emblazoned across the front. His jeans were worn and frayed on the hems. He stared at them through narrowed eyes. "What do you want?"

"Keme, right?" Amanda smiled gently. "I just want to talk with you," she said. "As the leader of the Young Wolves, I thought you might have some insight into the group. You know, how is everyone after losing three members?"

Keme lifted his chin toward Carter. "Who's the stiff with you?"

Amanda looked up at Carter and gave him a tight smile. "This is Carter Manning, my fiancé. He's driving me around until my car is back from the shop." She looked around at the little faces peering through the screen door. "Could we talk in private?"

Mrs. Hunting Horse moved closer to Keme. "What you have to say can be said in front of me. My boy doesn't keep secrets from his mama."

"I don't mean to keep any secrets, ma'am, but I don't think you want our discussion to be heard by little ears," Amanda nodded toward the children in the doorway.

Their mother turned and scowled at the children. "Get back to the table. I know you haven't finished eating."

"I've got this, mama," Keme said.

His mother met his gaze. "You sure? You know your daddy doesn't like it when strangers come on the property."

"We'll make it quick," Keme assured her. "Go on. Lucy and Tito will never finish their food without you watching over them."

She looked back at Amanda and Carter. "Don't stay too long. Keme's daddy will be home soon."

Carter stepped closer to Amanda and waited for

Mrs. Hunting Horse to go into the house, leaving Keme outside with Amanda and Carter.

Keme came down the steps, away from the door. "Why are you really here?" Keme asked in a hushed tone. "Did Tara send you?"

Amanda shook her head. "No, she didn't. She doesn't know we came."

Keme glared at her. "Then you've been talking to her? What did she say?"

"Only that Tobi didn't commit suicide," Amanda said, her voice low so as not to carry to the house.

"He didn't," Keme said. "Neither did Allison or Ryan."

"Then how did they die?" Carter asked.

Keme met his gaze. "I don't know. But they didn't commit suicide. And if they were on meth like they're saying, they didn't take it willingly."

"If not, then who gave it to them?" Amanda asked.

"What else did Tara say?" Keme demanded.

"Nothing. That's why we came to you. If someone is threatening you and the other members of the Young Wolves, you need to tell someone. If not me, then the police."

"No," Keme said, his eyes widening for a second before narrowing again. "I don't know of anyone threatening us. You need to leave now. My father will be home any minute. He doesn't like it when people show up here."

"Keme, if you know something that can stop

what's happening, tell us." Amanda reached out to touch the teen's arm.

The young man flinched and stepped away. "I don't know what you're talking about. Leave now. If you're not afraid of my father, then be aware of what he'll do to us for allowing you to stay as long as you have."

"That's it? You'll sacrifice every last one of your group members to keep a secret?" Amanda shook her head. "Tara is your girlfriend. Do you want to see what happened to her brother happen to her?"

"No," Keme spat out. "You can't understand."

"Then help us understand," Amanda said. "Tell us what's going on. Maybe we can help."

"You can't help." He shook his head. "You need to leave." He held out his arms and herded them toward Carter's truck. "Leave before—" He looked over their shoulders to the road behind them and muttered a curse. "Fuck. Now, you've gone and done it."

"Done what?" Amanda turned around, her eyes blinded by headlights heading their way.

Keme held up his hands. "I can't help you. You'll have to work this out on your own." He took several steps backward.

An orange pickup roared to a stop, kicking up dust and gravel.

The driver pushed open his door and climbed out, swaying slightly. "Who the hell are you, and why are you on my property?"

Carter turned to face the man. "You must be Oscar Hunting Horse."

"I sure as hell am, and you're trespassing. Get the hell off my property before I shoot you."

"We were just leaving," Amanda hooked her hand through the crook of Carter's arm. "Weren't we, darling?"

"We were." Carter didn't take his eyes off Oscar, who stood between them and Carter's truck, smelling of booze.

The man was big, mean and drunk. Not a good combination.

Carter steered Amanda wide of the angry Hunting Horse, hoping to get her out of there before the jerk did something stupid. "Sorry to disturb you."

"You'll be sorry, all right." Oscar cocked his arm and threw the first punch.

Carter gave Amanda a shove in the direction of the truck and brought his arm up to deflect the blow. Oscar's fist glanced off Carter's temple, barely grazing his skin.

The next time Oscar threw his fist, Carter was ready. He ducked the blow, grabbed the man's arm, twisted it around behind Oscar's back and shoved it up between his shoulder blades. "Amanda, get into the truck."

"But—"

"Get in the truck," he said between gritted teeth. "Mr. Hunting Horse and I are having a conversation."

"The hell we are," Oscar yelled. "Let me go."

"Not until you promise to behave." Carter watched Amanda get into the truck and close her door. Once she was securely inside, Carter loosened his hold on Oscar's arm at the same time as he gave the man a hefty shove, sending him flying forward.

Off-balance from the hold and the booze, Oscar hit the ground on his hands and his knees. He bellowed and came back up swinging.

Once again, Carter spun him around and jacked his arm up between his shoulder blades. "Are you going to quit swinging long enough for me to leave your property? Otherwise, I can stand here all night. Your choice. Take your time making your decision." He pushed the arm up higher, making the man rise on his toes to relieve the pain.

"Okay, okay, I won't swing again," Oscar called out.

"Don't fuck with me, Oscar," Carter whispered into the man's ear. "I'd hate to embarrass you in front of the women."

The man grunted for a few more seconds before finally saying, "I promise. I won't swing. Just get the hell off my place," he said, his voice strained.

"That's what we'll do." This time Carter gave the man a gentle push and released him.

Oscar spun to face him, rubbing his arm. "You have only as long as it will take me to get into my house and grab my gun to be gone."

"Take a shot at me or my fiancée, and I'll break both of your arms." Carter didn't move, holding Oscar's stare until the other man looked away.

Carter nodded toward Keme, turned and walked toward his truck. He fully expected Oscar to charge him from behind. The man must have realized Carter wouldn't tolerate another attack and left him alone.

Carter got into his truck, shifted into reverse and backed away from the house, watching Oscar the entire time.

The man stood where he'd left him, glaring.

When he felt he was far enough away from the toxic man, Carter spun the truck around and drove off the Hunting Horse property.

"Well," Amanda said, her voice breathy, "that went better than I expected. Though we don't know anything more than when we started."

"No, but one thing is certain." Carter glanced in his rearview mirror as the dilapidated house disappeared. "They're scared and probably into something that's way over their heads."

CHAPTER 7

"Where to?" Carter asked.

"It's getting late. As much as I'd hoped to get answers today, we'll have to wait until tomorrow to continue our investigation."

"Do you have a plan?"

She sighed. "I say we talk to every member of the Young Wolves until we find someone scared enough to talk."

"Oh, I think they're scared," Carter said. "Too scared to talk."

"That's what I'm afraid of. And we can't keep an eye on all of them."

She gave him directions to the little house she was living in at the end of one of the streets in town. Her backyard was a field of prairie grass with endless stars at night.

As Carter pulled to a stop in front of the little

cottage, it dawned on Amanda just how small the house was. It was fine for one lone woman with its one bedroom, one bathroom and a living room-kitchen combination.

She slipped out of the truck and fumbled for the keys in her pocket. When she tried to fit the key into the lock, she dropped it twice.

Carter scooped the key off the ground the second time it fell and slipped it into the lock. "It's going to be all right. I'll sleep on the couch."

She laughed. "I don't think so." Amanda walked into the little living room and tipped her head toward the couch that was no more than a love seat. Certainly not big enough to come close to accommodating Carter's length.

"I'll sleep on the couch," she said. "You can have the bed."

He shook his head. "I can sleep on the floor. I've slept in worse places."

She shook her head. "No. I can fit on the couch. You're helping me; the least you should get out of this is a decent night's sleep."

He took one step, closing the short distance between them, and pressed a finger to her lips. "Do you always argue?"

She stared up into his eyes, her mouth tingling from his touch. "No."

"Then accept that I'll sleep on the floor."

She nodded, her lips brushing against his finger,

sending ripples of sensation throughout her body. Amanda spun and dove into her bedroom, closing the door behind her.

She stood with her back to the door for a long time, willing her pulse to return to normal. When it finally did, she gathered her usual nightgown and stood in front of the door.

She liked to shower at night before going to sleep. But that meant stepping out of the bedroom to get to the bathroom—and facing him again.

Her pulse kicked into high gear again as she twisted the knob and opened the door.

She frowned.

The living room was empty.

When she turned toward the bathroom, the door opened, and Carter stepped out, wearing only his jeans, moisture dripping from his dark hair onto his naked chest.

Amanda's mouth went dry. She ran her tongue across parched lips and stared, unable to drag her gaze from his brawny physique.

"It's all yours," he said.

"Mine?" she whispered. His body was all hers? Amanda shook her head to clear the haze of lust. "Oh, the bathroom. Okay." Her cheeks burned. "I'll only be a few minutes."

"Do you have a couple of blankets I can use?" Carter asked.

"In the closet in the bedroom. Top shelf." She

ducked into the bathroom and closed the door, her face on fire. "Mine?" she muttered. "What did you think he meant, dumbass?"

"Did you say something?" Carter called out from the other side of the door.

Amanda clapped a hand to her mouth. "No." Under her breath, she added, "Nothing repeatable."

"I thought you were talking to me when you said dumbass."

"No, not you." Could she make a bigger fool of herself? "All me. Did you find the blankets?"

"Not yet," he responded. "I was more intrigued by the conversation you were having in the bathroom."

"Jerk," she murmured.

He chuckled. "I've been called worse."

His laugh made her reevaluate her stupid remark. Amanda shook her head, twisted the lock on the door and then untwisted it. Whatever happened would happen. Not that he would be so rude as to barge into the bathroom while she stood naked behind the shower curtain.

Maybe he would if she invited him in to join her.

"He's not that into you, Amanda."

"Do you always talk to yourself?" Carter asked through the thin door panel.

"As a matter of fact, I do." She pulled her blouse over her head and tossed it in the laundry basket. "I don't always have someone listening to my private conversations with myself." Unhooking her bra, she draped it over the towel rack, kicked off her shoes and shimmied out of her jeans and panties." As she stood naked in front of the mirror, she studied her reflection.

"Ah, who am I kidding? Your body is unremarkable."

"That's a matter of opinion," Carter said.

"Do you just have super hearing or something?" Amanda demanded.

"No, but I can hear everything you say, except when you actually whisper. Then I have to strain a little."

Amanda covered her private parts with both hands and realized how stupid that was when he was on the other side of the door and couldn't see it. "Anyone ever tell you it's rude to eavesdrop?"

"Anyone ever tell you your door does little to muffle sounds? In case you didn't remember, this room is so small I can hear a pin drop on the other side."

"Okay. Point made." She turned on the faucet to drown out the sounds of her continued muttering. Once the water was warm, she stepped into the shower and leaned her head back, letting the water wash away the worry and the road grime from the long day of travel. Had it only been one day since she'd driven out to West Yellowstone and back, spoken with Tara *and* had a run-in with Oscar Hunting Horse?

"No wonder I'm exhausted." She poured shampoo into her palm and lathered her hair. Using the suds from her hair, she spread them over her body and down between her legs.

Her core quivered and heated.

The door was unlocked. All she had to do was mention that fact to Carter and let him decide what he wanted to do. She opened her mouth to announce that the door was unlocked. Before she could, the hot water heater ran out of hot water, and she was hit with a blast of tepid to cool spray.

So much for inviting him into the shower with her.

She rinsed quickly, shut off the water and grabbed a towel. After drying off, she dressed in her nightgown and brushed the tangles out of her damp hair.

A glance in the mirror reminded her of just how thin the nightgown was. Amanda could see her nipples through the fabric. Great. She wouldn't have to announce that she was horny, her nipples would do the work for her.

Shoulders back, she marched out of the bathroom and immediately crossed her arms over her chest.

Carter had made a pallet of blankets on the floor and tossed one of the throw pillows from the couch onto the pile of blankets. He stood at the window with the blinds open, staring out at the night sky. "It's a beautiful night," he said.

"We have a lot of those on the Wind River Reservation. It's nice to be where you don't have to listen to traffic twenty-four-seven. Even nicer to see the stars. Most people who live in large metro areas also have to deal with light pollution. We have few security lights."

"A blessing and a curse, all in one?" Carter asked.

"Yes, it means people can get away with more under the cover of the dark." Amanda's mouth twisted. "Gang activity is rampant, and crime is ridiculously high."

Carter's mouth pressed into a thin line. "Sounds like paradise. Why stay?"

Amanda snorted. "They need help. Especially the young people who have their whole lives ahead of them. They need to know there are other choices besides crime, drugs and alcohol."

"That's a big job to tackle."

"Tell me about it." Amanda shook her head. "I can't even manage what's going on right now."

"You aren't the police or a detective. You shouldn't be tracking down a murderer."

"Our police force is horribly understaffed. The Medical Examiner and the Bureau of Indian Affairs are labeling the deaths as suicides. No one cares what happens to us."

"No one but you." Carter reached out to tuck a drying strand of her hair behind her ear. "You have beautiful hair," he said.

Her heart beat faster. "Thanks. When I was a teen,

I bleached it blond. I thought it would make people like me more." She shorted softly. "It didn't. I was still the foster kid from the rez the families had to put up with to get the additional money from the government. It took forever for my hair to grow out to its natural color."

Carter's brow wrinkled. He leaned back and studied her face and hair. "I can't picture you as a blonde. You look beautiful just the way you are."

No one had ever told her she was beautiful the way Carter said it.

Joe told her she was smart and looked good, and that she should be proud of her heritage.

Carter looked at her as if he were hungry and she was the meal.

Her heart racing, she was so very tempted to ask him to join her in her bed.

How wrong would that be? His job was to protect her, not make love to her. That would put him in an awkward position. The last thing she wanted was to be awkward with Carter.

Naked, yes.

Awkward, no.

With a sigh, she turned toward her bedroom. "I'm still willing to take the couch if you get tired of the cold, hard floor," she said over her shoulder.

"I'll be fine," he said. "Will you?"

She shot a narrow-eyed glance over her shoulder. "Why shouldn't I be?"

He shrugged, a smile tugging at the corners of his mouth. "No reason. I'll be here if you need me."

Her eyes narrowed more. Was she supposed to read something into his words? Geezus, she was terrible at flirting and sexual innuendo.

As she entered her room, she muttered to herself, "Why can't I just say it?"

"Say what?" he asked behind her.

"Nothing. Abso-freaking-lutely nothing."

He chuckled. "Did I make you mad?"

"No, of course not." She stood in the doorway to her bedroom, on the verge of…

Something.

"Have you ever been so knotted up inside you felt like you might explode?" she asked.

He nodded. "Many times."

"How did you loosen the knot?"

"Either by going for a run, or if a run was out of the question, I would say exactly what was on my mind. You know… get it off my chest. Are you feeling that way?" He crossed to stand in front of her. "Say what's on your mind, Amanda. You'll feel better."

"What if what's on my mind involves admitting to feelings someone else might not agree with?" She shook her head and started to turn. "Never mind."

Carter grabbed her wrist to keep her from walking away. "Say it, Amanda. If you don't, you'll be awake all night, wondering what would've happened if you had."

She loved how strong his hand was around her wrist and wished he was holding it pinned to the mattress while making love to her.

Amanda swallowed hard. If she said that out loud, he might laugh, or worse…feel sorry for her. "No. I can't," she whispered

"Then let me." He cupped her cheek in his hand and tipped her face up, forcing her to look into his soulful brown eyes. "You have eyes as black as the darkest night that sparkle when you're passionate about something. I've thought about your eyes all day and wondered how they'd sparkle in the throes of a different kind of passion…making love."

Her eyes rounded. "You have?"

He nodded. "After my wife was murdered, I swore I'd never give my heart to another woman. I'm not promising I'll give it to you. I'm not sure I can. But I can't ignore what my body is feeling when I'm close to you. I want to touch you. To feel your skin against mine. But I can't act on my feelings," he said.

Amanda met his gaze. "Why?"

"It wouldn't be fair to you. I can't promise you anything past the present. I won't lie to you and say I'll love you forever just to get you into bed." He brushed his lips across her forehead. "Ever since you nearly ran over me and Diablo and told me off because I was riding him too fast in a residential area, I've been all over the place with my feelings for you."

"You have?" she said, her pulse pounding so hard

against her eardrums she could barely hear herself think.

He nodded. "Angry, intrigued, impressed by your dedication to the teens, touched by how much you care about Tara and her family." His voice lowered. "And when your body brushes against me, my senses light up like the Fourth of July. Suddenly, I'm on fire. I want to hold you, touch you and feel your naked skin against mine." He laughed. "How's that for saying exactly what's on your mind? Now that it's off my chest, I should feel better."

"And do you?" she asked.

He frowned. "Not actually. I'm even more wound up and anxious to hear your response to my confession. Don't worry that you'll hurt my feelings. Tell me to go jump in a lake if I've read you wrong and you're not at all interested."

He backed a step, his brow descending. "Look, I didn't mean to put you on the spot. Forget what I just said. I'll just go back to my floor and sleep on it."

He turned away.

This time Amanda reached out and grabbed his wrist. "Hold up there. It's my turn to say what's on my mind. I'm the one who was so knotted up to begin with."

He lifted her hand up and pressed his lips to the backs of her knuckles. "Go on."

"You realize we haven't known each other for a full twenty-four hours, right?"

He nodded. "Time is just numbers."

"Is it right to feel the way we do?" She shook her head. "Love is something you build over time. What we're feeling is lust."

"So? What's wrong with lust? We're two consenting adults who can take care of ourselves. Why not act on what we're feeling?"

Amanda almost forgot how to breathe, her heart was beating so fast. "Yeah." She lifted her chin. "Why not?"

For a long moment, they stared into each other's eyes.

Amanda looked away first. "Or did we just make things awkward?"

"You think too much." Carter bent, scooped her up into his arms and carried her into the bedroom.

Amanda wrapped her arm around his neck and leaned in to kiss his chin. He turned his face and captured her mouth in a deep, swift kiss. Then he laid her on the bed, gripped the hem of her night-gown and dragged it up over her head. He stared down at her for a long moment, as if drinking her in.

Amanda reached up and wrapped her hand around the back of his neck, bringing his mouth down to hers.

He claimed her, his tongue pushing past her teeth to caress hers in sensuous thrusts until she was squirming beneath him, wanting more than just a kiss.

His mouth abandoned hers as he kissed a path down the length of her neck.

He shifted lower to capture one of her nipples and roll it gently between his teeth.

"Umm. Yes, I did think my nightgown was kind of sheer," she said, her voice a little breathless. Every time he touched her, she found it more difficult to suck air into her lungs. "Deep down, I suppose I hoped you'd notice as well."

"I did," he said and moved to claim the other nipple, flicking it with the tip of his tongue.

Amanda ran her hands over his shoulders, loving the feel of his skin beneath her fingertips and the strength of his muscles flexing with each movement.

Her core heated, the fire burning through her body, making her breathing labored and her desire flare to a fevered pitch.

Carter moved lower, his mouth blazing a trail over her ribs and down to the elastic of her panties.

He hooked his finger in the band and dragged them down her legs, pressing a kiss to the inside of her thigh on his way down. Once he'd divested her of the last bit of clothing, he returned to the patch of hair covering her sex.

When he paused, she held her breath, waiting for what he would do next, eager to take it to the next level.

Carter parted her folds with his thumbs and blew a stream of warm air over clit.

Amanda leaned back, letting her body take over, her mind lost in the moment.

He touched her there with the tip of his tongue, igniting the nerves tightly packed into that little nubbin of flesh.

Amanda dug her fingers into his hair, holding him there, silently begging him to do it again.

When he did, she brought her knees up and dug her heels into the mattress. "Yes," she murmured.

The third time he flicked her clit, she arched her back and raised her hips. "Oh, yes," she cried.

He chuckled as he swirled his tongue around that magic place and slid a finger inside her channel.

By that time, Amanda was past thinking and fully into feeling every electric current bolting through her veins, the tension mounting inside to a jagged peak.

Another flick of his tongue sent her flying over the edge, the sensations shooting through her like a steady stream of fireworks, launching one after the other to the grand finale.

She rode the wave of feelings to the very end and drifted back to earth, spent yet sated. And oddly hungry for more.

Tightening her fingers in his hair, she tugged gently, urging him to come up to lie between her legs.

He leaned over her, his cock nudging her entrance, her juices coating the tip.

"I want you," she said. "Inside me. Now."

"Hold that thought." Carter rolled off her and stood.

Only then did she realize he was still wearing his jeans.

But not for long. He dug into his back pocket for his wallet, took out a foil packet and tossed it onto the pillow beside her. Then he shucked his jeans in one fluid motion.

He stood before her completely naked, his cock jutting forward, full, thick and ready.

Amanda licked her lips, sat up on the bed and wrapped her fingers around his length. Velvety softness encased his hard shaft. She ran her fingers from the tip to the base where she fondled his balls, rolling them in her palms. Then she leaned close and kissed the tip, sliding her tongue across the tiny hole and around the rim.

His cock jerked in reaction to her touch. He smoothed his hands over her hair and cupped the back of her head, urging her closer.

Amanda took him into her mouth, slowly easing over him, taking his full length until he nudged the back of her throat. All the while, she circled him with her tongue, stroking and flicking the length of him.

He pulled out to the very tip.

Amanda captured his buttocks in her hands and brought him back into her mouth. He eased out and back in, settling into a smooth rhythm, increasing the pace with each stroke until he was moving in and out so fast, she barely had time to take a breath.

His body stiffened, and he pulled free.

Amanda lay back on the bed, her knees falling to each side, laying her open to him.

She took the foil packet, tore it open and removed the condom, rolling it over his engorged staff.

Then he was between her legs, his cock pressing against her entrance.

She gripped his hips and guided him home, taking his full length inside. He filled her completely, so thick and long.

For a moment, he paused, letting her channel adjust to his girth, then he was moving again, sliding in and out, faster and faster. His body grew rigid, and his face tightened until he thrust one last time, hard and deep.

Amanda wrapped her legs around his waist and held him inside her as his cock pulsed his release.

When he came back down, he lay on top of her for a moment, crushing the air from her lungs.

Amanda didn't care if she died right then. Making love with Carter had been perfection.

He gathered her in his arms, rolled to the side and took her with him, without severing their intimate connection. For a long time, he held her close, their naked flesh pressed together.

Amanda rested her cheek against his chest and an arm around his middle. "I like this."

"Me, too."

"Better than sleeping on the floor?"

"Much," he said and settled his chin on top of her head.

Exhausted from everything that had happened from the time she'd left early that morning to minutes before making love with a man she'd just met, Amanda yawned. "Are we going to be all awkward and weird tomorrow?" She closed her eyes, content to be in the moment.

"Only if you let yourself be awkward." He softly stroked her hair. "What happened here was…amazing. Nothing awkward about that."

She nodded with her eyes still closed. "I'm glad you're not sleeping on the floor."

He pressed a kiss to her forehead. "Me, too."

Amanda knew she couldn't expect a repeat performance from Carter. He'd been clear that he wouldn't give his heart to another.

But damn. Amanda prayed what had happened between them wouldn't be a one-night stand. It was worthy of an encore. She drifted to sleep with a smile on her face, looking forward to waking up to Carter in her bed.

She'd barely gotten to sleep when the sharp sound of glass breaking, jerked her upright.

Carter was out of the bed and halfway across the room before Amanda realized what was happening.

The roar of engines filled the night outside her little cottage.

Amanda slipped out of her bed, dragging the top sheet with her. She wrapped it around her body and peeked through the blinds.

Eight to ten motorcycles circled the cottage.

"Stay away from the window," Carter called out. "And don't turn on a light."

He stood naked in the doorway to her bedroom, reached into the next room and grabbed his boots. After he pulled on his boots, he hurried into the living room and grabbed his leather jacket. From one of the pockets, he pulled out a handgun.

Amanda shivered at the sight of Carter easing up to the broken window. Something hard hit the side of the house. Moments later, the glass in the bedroom window exploded. A heavy rock landed in the middle of her bed along with shards of the broken window.

"Unless you can reach your shoes, don't move," Carter said. "There's glass all over the floor."

"I'm staying put," Amanda promised. "I think my shoes are on the other side of the bed. I could go over the bed to get to them."

"Don't risk it," Carter said. "We don't know how much debris could've made it onto your bed."

"At least one massive rock," Amanda muttered. "Where it landed, it would have hit one of us in the head had we still been asleep." Amanda shivered. "What do they want?"

"By the look of it, they want to scare you."

Amanda snorted. "They're doing a good job of it."

"Looks like they're leaving," Carter said. "The leader just took off down the street. The others are following."

A few moments later, the block returned to its quiet norm. Other than the broken windows and glass littering the floor, it could have been any other night.

Amanda pulled herself up into the bed, the sheet still wrapped around her body. "Who were they?"

"Based on the tattoos I saw on one of the riders, I'd bet it was the NA Syndicate." He entered her bedroom, found Amanda's shoes and handed them to her.

She slipped her feet into the shoes and stood on the floor. "I need to see how much damage they did."

"You might want to put on some clothes," he said with a crooked grin. "You don't want to get caught with your sheet down."

"Yeah, I definitely don't want to lose my sheet," she responded, tongue-in-cheek.

Carter laughed. "I'm glad to see you haven't lost your sense of humor."

"What else do I have?" she said. "Teens are dying around me, and my house has been vandalized. What more could happen?"

CHAPTER 8

CARTER TOUCHED a finger to her lips. "Shh. Don't invite trouble to find us." He reached up and knocked on the wood trim around the bedroom doorframe. "I hope that was enough to keep bad things from happening."

Amanda cocked an eyebrow in his direction. "You're a Navy SEAL. I assumed you wouldn't believe in superstition, tarot cards, mind-reading or other woo-woo stuff."

"I believe in luck," Carter said. "Good and bad luck. I also believe you can pull yourself out of a bad luck situation if you try hard enough. But you don't tempt fate."

"You speak as if from the experience of having tempted fate."

He grinned. "I knew a guy deployed into heavy

fighting in a small village in Afghanistan. It was his last mission before he redeployed to the States. He carried a half-dozen rabbits' feet in his pocket. He gave them away to some of the children of the village. Next thing I heard, he was shot and killed by a lone Taliban gunman."

Amanda cocked an eyebrow. "So, what you're telling me is that he should've kept at least one of his lucky rabbits' feet?"

"I'm just saying, he might've survived if he'd held onto at least one lucky rabbit's foot," Carter said. "By you saying what more could happen... you've set us up for more."

Amanda's cell phone vibrated against the night-stand. Her heart sank to the bottom of her belly. "Do you think I jinxed us?"

"Only one way to find out." Carter picked it up and handed it to Amanda.

"Now, I'm afraid to answer it." Her hand shook as she held the device.

"Answer before the last ring," Carter urged. "Better to know what you're up against than to walk around without a clue."

Amanda answered the unknown number. "Hello." She listened, the color draining from her face. "A coma?" She looked up, her gaze meeting Carter's. "We'll be right there." She ended the call and faced Carter, her face ashen. "That was 911 dispatch. Joe's at the Riverton hospital in ICU. They found him in a ditch on the side of the road, several yards from his service vehicle."

"What happened?" Carter asked.

"It looked like he made a traffic stop, and they beat him up using a stick, baseball bat or something else hard. He had blunt force trauma all over his head and body. They aren't sure he's going to make it." Tears welled in her eyes as she hurried to pull on a pair of jeans, a bra and a blouse.

Carter wanted to drag the woman into his arms and hold her tightly to ease the pain. Now wasn't a good time to do that.

He dressed and waited by the door. They left the little house only to find his truck had been vandalized along with the house. They'd spraypainted NA on the sides of the house and Carter's truck in bright red paint.

Amanda clamped a hand over her mouth as she climbed into his truck. "I'm so sorry I got you into this."

Though it pissed him off that a gang had tagged his truck, it made him even angrier that they'd targeted Amanda and the tribal police chief. "I'm not worried about a little paint. I'm more worried that they're threatening you and Joe. You aren't safe here."

"Neither are the teens I'm supposed to help." She stared out the window as Carter pulled away from the little house at the end of the street. "I can't leave them to fight this battle alone."

"You can't fight a battle where you're greatly outnumbered," Carter said.

Amanda banged her fist against the armrest, her face set, her eyes blazing. "There has to be a way to end this. I won't walk away, and I won't be driven away by a bunch of thugs. They want a war…I'll give them one."

"One woman against a gang of dozens. And if this is all about drug trafficking, you could be up against a drug ring of thousands." Carter shook his head. "You're in way over your head."

"We could get the Bureau of Indian Affairs to help," she offered.

"They might be in up to their eyeballs, giving the gangs and drug runners free rein on the reservation for a kickback."

"Then we have to do it on our own." She glanced his way. "They almost killed Joe. He was only doing his job." She threw her hands in the air. "He might still die. Then that will be another murder to add to the other three. Only they won't be able to call this one a suicide. Nobody beats himself in the head and body until he's comatose."

The gray light of dawn spread over the landscape as they arrived in Riverton and pulled into the hospital parking lot.

Amanda was out of the truck and running for the entrance before Carter brought the truck to a complete halt. He shifted into park, dropped down from his seat and ran to catch up with her as she reached the sliding glass doors.

The receptionist at the Emergency Room desk gave them the directions to the Intensive Care Unit and assured them Joe Sharp Spear was being taken care of there.

Amanda stood silent on the ride up the elevator.

Carter reached for her hand and held it as the door opened.

Nurses rolled computer carts from room to room, logging vital signs or dispensing medication.

One sat at the station, her fingers clicking across a keyboard, her attention on the monitor in front of her. When her hands stilled, she glanced up with a smile. "Can I help you?"

"We're here to see Joe Sharp Spear," Amanda said.

"Are you relatives of Mr. Sharp Spear?" the nurse asked.

Amanda nodded. "I'm his daughter."

The nurse tipped her head to the left. "You'll find him in the second room on your right. The doctor came in early this morning. He hasn't regained consciousness since they brought him in. You'll have to speak with the doctor for a full description of his injuries and the treatment plan."

Amanda nodded. "Thank you." Holding tightly to Carter's hand, she walked down the corridor, slowing as she reached the second door on the right.

The hallway walls were glass, allowing the nurses

to see into the room. The door stood open. A monitor beeped with every beat of Joe's heart, only slightly reassuring.

The man lay in a sea of white sheets, his dark face even darker with bruising. A white bandage swathed his head, and his eyes were so swollen he couldn't have opened them if he'd wanted.

Amanda's hand squeezed Carter's hard. "What kind of animal does this to another human being?" She entered the room and went to the side of the bed, releasing Carter's hand to gently touch an uninjured portion of Joe's arm. "Joe? It's me, Amanda. I'm here for you, Joe. You're going to be all right." Her voice cracked, and tears rolled down her cheeks. "I'm going to make things right. Whoever did this won't get away with it."

Carter didn't bother to remind her that Joe was in a coma and probably couldn't hear anything she was saying. If there was any possibility he could, it might help him to hold on and fight to come back from the horrifically brutal attack.

Carter moved a chair close to the side of the bed and urged Amanda to sit while she talked to Joe and stroked his arm. There wasn't anything he could do to ease the pain of seeing a loved one lying so near to death. The best thing he could do was to be there for her.

An hour later, the doctor came by to check on Joe. He shined a light into Joe's eyes and read through the charts. Finally, he turned to Amanda. "You're Mr. Sharp Spear's daughter?"

She nodded. "Foster daughter. Joe doesn't have any other family."

"We had to do emergency surgery to stop some internal bleeding. His x-rays show broken ribs and a break in the right forearm. We'll set the arm in a cast today. His ribs will heal on their own. The CT scan indicated a small linear fracture in the skull. We didn't detect any bleeding, but the fact he's been unconscious since they brought him in is concerning. We'd like to keep him in ICU one more night at least."

Amanda nodded. "What are the chances of him recovering fully?"

The doctor shrugged. "We won't know until he wakes up and we can perform a neurological exam to determine if there is any brain damage. Right now, it's a waiting game."

"He has to wake up," Amanda said softly, her gaze on Joe's battered face.

"That's right," the doctor said. "He's in good hands with the ICU nurses. They'll let me know when he wakes up." The doctor left the room to finish his rounds.

Carter's cell phone vibrated in his pocket. He pulled it out and noted the call was from Stone Jacobs. "I need to answer this," he told Amanda and stepped out of the room. He walked to the end of the hall and stopped in front of a window before he answered. "This is Carter."

"Kyla and I made it to Fort Washakie," Stone announced. "Where do you want us to leave Amanda's car?"

"For now, leave it at the Wind River Police Station," Carter said. "Amanda and I are at the hospital in Riverton. The chief of tribal police was attacked last night and left for dead in a ditch."

"This the man who was Amanda's foster parent?" Stone asked.

"Yes, sir." He filled him in on what had happened to Joe and the attack on the cottage where Amanda lived.

"Sounds like you need more help." Stone said.

"This problem is bigger than just a couple of kids committing suicide," Carter said. "The attacks last night were clearly a warning to back off."

"I don't like it," Stone said. "You and Amanda can't stop an all-out war all by yourselves."

Carter's grip tightened on his cell phone. "I'm not sure this aggression *can* be stopped."

"It has to be drug-related," Stone said. "I had a call from Hank's computer guy, Swede. He said he found evidence that there's an ongoing investigation into drug trafficking in the area. In fact, they have a DEA agent embedded, undercover, at the Wind River Reservation. We don't want to step on their toes if they're working on an operation."

"Did Swede get the name of the agent?" Carter asked.

"His real name is Matt Jones, but he won't be using that name on the rez. Supposedly, he's gone deep undercover."

Carter ran a hand through his hair. "It would be nice to know who he is."

"Yeah," Stone said. "We could be working together to help locate the man managing the flow of drugs coming up from Mexico."

"No kidding." Carter shook his head. "In the meantime, teens are dying, the police chief could die, and Amanda is being targeted for asking too many questions."

"They don't want you, Amanda, the tribal police or a few teenagers to put a crimp in the flow of product to the users."

"That's a given," Carter agreed.

"What we need is to find out who's spearheading the flow and take him out. He has to be dealing directly with the Mexican cartel that's providing the product. I'd read where the cartel targets reservations because the people are among the most vulnerable. They get them hooked on meth and the ones they hook become their local dealers."

"Isn't the DEA supposed to be finding the source?"

"Could be harder than they thought. Or it takes

time to trace the drugs back to the source," Stone said.

Carter snorted. "Whoever the source is, they have the backing of the local gang to apply muscle when their supply chain is threatened."

"This could be a huge can of worms."

"Yeah." Carter sighed. "Amanda isn't giving up on her people. She's in it for the long haul, unless they take her out first."

Stone shoved a hand through his hair. "Let me touch bases with Hank and see what he suggests. In the meantime, do you want me and Kyla to stick around? You might need someone to cover your six."

Carter laughed. "That's funny that you think I need protection when I'm here to protect Amanda. Like you said, it's a huge can of worms. Hank might not want to get that involved. For now, I want the NA Syndicate to think we're backing down. If you show up to add to our numbers, they'll know we're not letting it go."

"Okay then. We'll leave Amanda's car at the station and head back to West Yellowstone until we have a plan. But I want you to remember, you're not in this alone. You have the full backing of the Brotherhood Protectors. We're a team."

"Good to know. I might need you sooner than later," Carter said and ended the call.

Amanda rose from her chair when he entered Joe's room.

"That was Stone Jacobs. He and Kyla are dropping your car at the police station. I figured it was safer there than at your house."

She nodded. "Yes. I might be camping at the police station until this situation gets resolved."

Carter moved closer and lowered his voice so only Amanda could hear. "Stone said Hank's computer guy found out there's a DEA operative working the Wind River Reservation undercover."

Amanda's eyes widened. "Good. We need to talk to him."

"The problem is, he's undercover. He could have embedded in the NA Syndicate for all we know. He's not going to break cover to talk to us."

Amanda frowned. "Surely, we can figure out who he is and corner him for some answers."

"If we can figure out who he is," he said, shaking his head.

"If someone wants to live on the reservation, they have to register with the tribal council. We could check the registry for newer names."

"Good idea," Carter glanced at Joe. "Are you ready to go?"

Amanda turned to Joe, leaned over and brushed a feathery kiss across his cheek. "I love you, Joe. I'll be back as soon as I can. In the meantime, try to restrain yourself from flirting with the pretty nurses." She smiled, her eyes glazed with tears. "And please, get better soon."

Amanda left the room and went straight to the nurses' station. "Please, have hospital security come up to this floor."

The nurse frowned. "Why?"

"Some people tried to kill Joe Sharp Spear," Amanda said. "They could come back to finish the job."

"They might hurt anyone who gets in their way, including hospital staff," Carter added.

"Seriously?" The nurse's eyes widened. "I'll get right on it." She picked up the phone and contacted security.

Amanda waited until she was certain someone would be on guard duty while Joe was still in the hospital.

When a hospital security guard finally arrived, Amanda held out her hand to Carter.

He took it and gently squeezed her fingers.

"I'm glad you're with me," she said. "I don't think I could do this on my own."

"I'm not sure you can do this with just me. I think we need an entire Army."

Amanda's mouth formed a thin, tight line. "We'll find a way to take back the reservation. These people cannot be allowed to get away with what they're doing." With her shoulders held back and a fierce glare in her eyes, Amanda walked with Carter to the elevator.

She was beautiful with her dark hair hanging

straight down her back, her high cheekbones and rounded jaw set and those amazing blue eyes blazing.

Carter's chest swelled. He could see the warrior in her. "You never told me, are you Arapaho or Shoshoni?" he asked as they exited the elevator.

She cast a glance in his direction. "Does it matter?"

"To you, maybe. To me? Only if it matters to you. I'm just curious."

"I work with all the teens on the reservation, Arapaho, Shoshoni, Hispanic, Asian or white," she said. "Everyone should be treated with respect and fairness."

"I agree." He bit back a grin at the fact she hadn't answered his question. He wouldn't push it. If she wanted him to know, she'd tell him.

Her lips twitched, and she shot a glance his way. "Northern Arapaho."

He smiled. "Not that it makes a difference about how I feel about you, but thank you. It's an important part of who you are. That means something to me."

"And how do you feel about me?" she asked as he held the passenger door open for her.

He bent and pressed a kiss to her lips. "I think you're amazing."

She leaned up on her toes and pressed her lips to his, returning the kiss. "You're not so bad yourself."

He grinned. "See? No awkwardness whatsoever."

Her cheeks flushed a ruddy pink beneath the

natural darkness of her skin. "Maybe just a little." She climbed up into the seat and buckled her seatbelt.

He gave her a crooked grin. "That will improve the more we get to know each other." Carter closed the door and rounded the truck to the driver's side, refusing to get angry all over again at the bright red paint marring the shiny black paint. They had bigger problems.

As he slid behind the steering wheel, Amanda's cell phone chirped.

She pulled it from her pocket and frowned. "Not sure who it is." She answered, "This is Amanda."

Carter strained to hear the voice on the cell phone. All he could tell was that it was female.

"Slow down, Tara," Amanda said. "The NA Syndicate? How do you know?" Her eyes narrowed. "The bastards! Are you in a safe place now?"

Carter met Amanda's gaze as she spoke with the teen.

"And your family?" Amanda shook her head. "Go to the Wind River Police Station and stay there until I can get you some help. Don't leave. You know you can't go to Keme. His family situation isn't going to help yours. Your mother and siblings need you to stay with them. Please, Tara, go to the police station and wait for me to get there. Call me and let me know all four of you are there and safe. Promise me." Amanda held the cell phone against her ear for several long seconds. "Thank you. Now, go."

When the call ended, Amanda lifted her chin toward the road. "We need to get back to Fort Washakie. The same jerks who attacked my house, and probably attacked Joe, went after Tara and her family."

Carter whipped the truck into drive and pulled out onto the road, heading back the way they'd come. "They need to get somewhere safe," he said.

"Sadly, that's not on the reservation." Amanda's brow knit in a deep frown. "They have to leave until we can get a handle on who's behind this rash of terrorism."

"I might have a temporary solution for Tara's family." Carter pulled his phone out of his pocket and called Stone. "You still in Fort Washakie?"

"Yes, we are," Stone responded. "What's up?"

"I need you to go to the police station and wait for a small family that will be arriving soon. One of them is the twin to the latest dead teen, Tara Running Fox. Her family is being targeted. We need to get them off the reservation to somewhere safe until we can resolve this situation."

"Got it. They can stay at the lodge in West Yellowstone for the time being."

"They don't have any way to pay for their lodging. Tara's mother works two jobs just to put food on the table and pay utilities."

"Don't worry about it," Stone said. "They can stay there free. I've given Hank the head's up that we might need more help than even his organization can provide. He's working it from his end."

"As long as he keeps it on the down low. We don't know who we're dealing with. What if this organization has ties to the government? They might catch wind of what we're doing here and alert their leader and the main players. We can't let any of them get away."

"You have a point. They'd just wait for the smoke to clear and go back to business as usual," Stone said. "Hank's smart, and he has connections he trusts.

"Let's hope they're trustworthy. Our lives and the lives of others are at risk."

"Roger," Stone said. "Kyla and I are back at the station. We'll be looking for the Running Fox family. I'll give Hank a call and let him know we're evacuating the family to a safer location."

"Thanks, Stone. We should be back in Fort Washakie in less than twenty minutes."

"We might head out before you get here."

"Understood. I'll have Amanda call Tara and let her know to expect to find you and Kyla." He ended the call and turned to Amanda. "Call Tara and let her know Stone and Kyla are there and will get them to a safe location."

Amanda called Tara's number and waited. "I'm not getting a response. I'm not getting a ringtone either." She tried again and shook her head. "Nothing."

He reached over and covered her hand, giving her a reassuring smile. "They might be in an area with limited cell phone reception. Give them a minute or two before trying again."

"You're right. Reception on the rez is sketchy at best." She stared at her cell phone for the next two minutes. Just when she started to call Tara's number again, her phone rang.

"This is Amanda," she said in a rush. Her tight lips loosened into a relieved smile. "Tara, thank goodness. You're where?" Amanda gave Carter a thumbs-up. "Good. When you pull in, there will be a couple there. Stone Jacobs and his fiancé, Kyla. They're good friends of my fiancé. They're going to get you and your family to somewhere safe until this blows over."

Amanda listened, nodding. "I know you don't want to leave Keme and the others, but you need to go with your family and help your mother with the younger kids. They need you now more than ever. If we don't get there before you leave, know I'm thinking about you. I'm glad you're getting away."

She listened again. "Oh good. You can trust them. They're the good guys. And once you get away from here, if you want to tell me anything, you can call me day or night."

When the call ended, Amanda turned to Carter. "They made it to the station and found Stone and Kyla."

"Great. They'll make sure they get out of town safely."

Amanda drew in a deep breath and let it out slowly. "With Tara out of harm's way, that's one less person I have to worry about." Her shoulders slumped. "There are still so many more who could be hurt. We have to help them, and evacuating everyone, like we're doing with Tara, is not an option. She did tell me it was the NA Syndicate who attacked their place. She recognized the leader."

"Who is the leader?" Carter asked.

"Trevor Spotted Elk." Amanda's lips pressed into a straight line. "We can head for the tribal council and start the search for our undercover DEA agent. And while we're there, I'll tap into my tribal network and see where we can find Trevor Spotted Elk."

CHAPTER 9

AMANDA WAS first through the door at the Tribal Council's building, where they kept records of the decedents of the Northern Arapaho and Eastern Shoshoni tribes.

"Hi, Wanda," she called out to the woman seated behind a desk. "How are you today?"

The older woman looked up from her computer and smiled. "Amanda, it's good to see your pretty face." Her smile faded. "I heard about Joe. Have you been to see him? Is he going to be okay?"

Amanda nodded. "I went to the hospital in Riverton. He's still in a coma. The doctor won't know anything until he regains consciousness."

Wanda rose from her seat and came around to hug Amanda. "I'm so sorry. I know he means a lot to you. He means a lot to all of us. He's so selfless in his service to the reservation. I'll be thinking about him, sending him healing thoughts."

"Thank you." Amanda gave Wanda a watery smile. "Joe's a tough guy. If anyone can come back from what he went through, he can."

"That's right." Wanda looked to Carter. "Are the rumors true?" She reached for Amanda's left hand and grinned at the ring. "You're engaged?"

Heat filled Amanda's cheeks. "Yes, I am." She turned to Carter. "This is Carter Manning, my fiancé."

Wanda shook Carter's hand. "Congratulations. You're getting a wonderful girl. Amanda has a huge heart. She cares so much for our people and is making a difference with our teens."

"I wish I could say I was," Amanda said. "They're so easily swayed by the wrong people."

Wanda clucked her tongue. "I know. So many of them are joining gangs and doing drugs. But if you can save even one, you're making a difference." She smiled from Amanda to Carter and back. "I'm sure you didn't come in just to visit me, though you're welcome anytime. What can I do for you?"

"Wanda, we'd like to look at the registry of people who've come to live on the reservation in the past year or two."

"Looking for anyone in particular?" she asked as she brought up a computer screen and turned it toward Amanda. "We have had a few people return from other states after long absences. It's always nice to see our people come home."

"I'm not sure what I'm looking for," Amanda admitted. "I just want to get an idea of who came to live here in case I'm missing a teen or young adult I should be helping." Amanda felt a twinge of guilt that lying was getting to be easier. She should have felt worse about it, but she was looking for the good of her people. Finding the DEA agent could help. She needed to talk to the man. Maybe he had some insight into what was happening.

The other person she wanted to talk with had a name. "Wanda, you wouldn't happen to know how I can get in touch with Trevor Spotted Elk, would you?" If anyone knew where to find someone on the reservation, it was Wanda Morning Light.

Wanda frowned. "Mona Spotted Elk's boy?"

Amanda nodded. "Yes, ma'am."

"He's not a teen. Hasn't been in a while."

"I know, but he connects with a lot of teens and has some influence over them."

Wanda snorted. "Not in a good way. You would be better off steering clear of that young man. He's bad news to the reservation."

"Still," Amanda said, "I'd like to talk with him and get an understanding of what motivates teens to follow a guy like that."

"Then the safest place to catch him is at his job."

Amanda raised her eyebrows. "Job?"

Wanda's lips pinched together. "I'll never understand why, but he landed a job at the casino in security. If you corner him there, hopefully, he'll behave himself. He would have to. The casino is equipped with cameras monitoring the gamblers and the staff. He's probably there now until later this evening. I think he works the evening shift until around midnight."

Amanda caught Carter's gaze. That added up to tagging her house around 2:00 am.

"I can print that list of those folks who have come in over the past two plus years." Wanda turned the monitor back toward her desk chair and sat behind it. "It will only take me a minute to get that for you." Her fingers flew over the keyboard, and she hit enter with a flourish and a smile. "Check the printer." She pointed to the printer in the corner of the office.

Amanda crossed to the corner where the printer spat out a sheet of paper. She took it and smiled at Wanda. "Thank you."

"That's just the names, ages and how they qualify to be here. I have addresses, though they might not be current. They only give them to me when they register to live on the reservation. Some folks don't bother to register and move in with relatives."

And some people who didn't belong moved in— people who didn't want the authorities to know where they were. With over 2.2 million acres of reservation, a person could get lost.

With pathetically few law enforcement personnel, between the Wind River Police Department and the Bureau of Indian Affairs Police, they couldn't begin to keep track of everything going on.

To Amanda, teens dying suspicious deaths made the situation critical. She held up the page. "I'll let you know if I need more information. Thank you."

"I hope you don't get attitude from Trevor. He might be able to charm teens into doing what he wants, but I've known people who got on his bad side." Her brow furrowed. "Let's just say I knew people who were on his bad side. I wouldn't be surprised if he had something to do with what happened to Joe and the damage to your house. He's bad news."

"Why would they hire a man like that at the casino?" Amanda asked, not really expecting an answer.

"I think it was more to keep the staff in line than the guests."

"That could be the case." It made sense to Amanda. The reservation residents fortunate to secure employment at the casino would know Trevor's reputation. Guests came in from Utah, Colorado, Montana and more just to gamble. They wouldn't know Trevor was a thug to be wary of. "Wanda, thank you for the information and the advice."

She frowned. "When Joe comes around, you tell him I'm thinking about him. And I hope you two will be okay. Given last night's attacks, I worry about you both. Most likely, it was a warning. Whatever you're doing pissed off someone."

Amanda nodded. "Yeah, and they piss me off."

Wanda stared hard at Amanda. "Be careful. Some people play for keeps." She shifted her gaze to Carter. "Keep a close eye on her if you want her to make it to the wedding."

Carter tipped his head. "Yes, ma'am." His hand came up to rest at the small of Amanda's back. He bent and brushed a kiss against Amanda's temple. "You ready, dear?"

Desire flared from each point he touched, reminding her of what they'd shared the night before. Heat burned at her core. She leaned into his body. "I'm ready." For a repeat of last night, before the gang had trashed her house and Joe had been attacked.

Carter led her out of the council building and to the passenger side of his pickup. He held the door for her and helped her up into her seat. "Are you sure you want to confront Trevor Spotted Elk?"

The desire of moments before froze in her veins. Her lips pressed into a tight line. "Now, more than ever. If he's responsible for what happened to Joe and what's happening to the teens," she clenched her fists, "I will take him down. One way or another. He can't get away with murder. I don't care how scary he is. He can't get away with what he's done."

"You're only one person. With me, that makes it

two. You saw the gang outside your house in the dark. They were probably hitting Joe at the same time. I'm thinking at least a dozen minions are working with whoever is doing this."

"Probably more. The young people and unemployed have nothing else to do on this reservation. They like to belong to something. Gangs give them a sense of belonging, and there is power in numbers."

"You think we can take down an entire gang?" Carter snorted. "Ask the Chicago police how that's working for them. Or the LAPD. And there are more of them than you, me and all of the law enforcement personnel on the reservation."

Amanda faced Carter. "You saw Tara. She's scared. She's already lost her brother. And she's not alone." Amanda turned back to stare out the front windshield and spoke softly. "I imagine the rest of the Young Wolves are afraid to step outside. No, they're probably scared to death to go home and take their troubles to their families."

This problem went deeper than one person or even two. It would take a huge effort, maybe even an army of people, to clean up the gangs on the reservation. Amanda didn't want him to leave, but he was right. They couldn't do it alone. She had to give him the opportunity to back out before it got any more dangerous than it already was.

"You don't have to go with me," she said. "I'll understand if you want out. I won't think less of you if you leave me at my car and drive back to West Yellowstone. You could tell Stone I fired you, and I decided to go it alone."

CARTER SLOWED THE TRUCK, pulled to the side of the road and shifted into park. Anger burned in his veins, making him want to…

He reached across the console, popped Amanda's seatbelt loose and let it retract.

Her eyes rounded. "Do you want me to get out here?" With her hand on the door handle, she waited for his response.

Instead of words, he grabbed the hand closest to him and stopped her from getting out. "No. I don't want you to get out." Carter pulled her across to sit on his lap and held her close, burying his hands in her thick black hair. "I will not drop you at your car and let you do this alone. I will not drive back to West Yellowstone and forget I ever met you or any of the people on this reservation. I'm in this whether you want me here or not."

"I want you here," she whispered, "but I don't want you hurt."

"I want you out of here so you won't get hurt. But I know you won't let this go. It's who you are and one of the reasons I'm doing something I never thought I'd do again in my life."

She stared into his eyes. "Do what?" Her brow knit. "Hit me? Swear at me?" Tears welled. "Kiss me?"

He claimed her mouth in a hard, almost brutal kiss.

Damn her.

He wanted to hate what she was doing to him. Wanted to be able to walk away, not feeling a thing.

But he couldn't. In one day, she'd crawled under his skin, and he couldn't walk away.

She clung to him, her hands lacing around his neck, her tongue pushing past his teeth to war with his.

He couldn't get enough of her, and yet she was too much. The feelings she made him feel threatened to overwhelm him.

Finally, he released her lips and crushed her to his chest, his lips pressed to her temple, her dark hair tickling his nose. "Damn you," he whispered.

"Why?" she said.

"For making me feel things I never wanted to feel again."

"Like?"

"Fear."

She captured his face in her palms. "Are you afraid of Trevor?"

He shook his head. "No. I'm afraid of losing you. I lost someone I loved before. I didn't ever want to feel that kind of pain again."

"But you barely know me," she said. "And yet, I feel like I've known you my entire life."

"Exactly." He cupped her cheek and brushed a thumb across her swollen lips. "I shouldn't feel so connected to you. Not so soon. Hell, not at all. I don't want to fall in love." He leaned his forehead against hers. "If we're together much longer, I may not have a choice."

She chuckled. "Hey, I didn't even like you when I first saw you. I keep asking myself what happened to make me like you so much. So, what if we were stupid enough to fall in love? Is that such a bad thing?"

He leaned back and stared into her eyes. "I've been shot at, injured and surrounded by the enemy. Nothing scared or hurt me more than when my commanding officer told me that my wife had been murdered at home, alone in our bed."

"If you had to do it all over again, would you have married her?"

He didn't hesitate. "Yes. I loved her."

"Knowing you would lose her to a murderer?" Amanda asked softly. "You would miss the love you had, miss the memories you made all because you wouldn't want the pain her death brought…"

He stared into her eyes, seeing the memories of the years he'd had with his wife flash through his mind. "No. I cherish those memories."

"Then why would you deny yourself happiness?

We don't know what life will throw our way. We have to live in the present, love while we can and stock up on memories." She pressed a kiss to his lips. "You don't have to fall in love with me. But let yourself love again. You deserve to love and be loved."

He held her close, letting her words sink in. "I don't know if I could stand to lose another person I love."

"Maybe you won't lose her. Maybe you'll grow old together with a dozen grandchildren scattered around you." She smiled into his eyes. "The point is, don't stop living because someone you loved died."

He gave her a weak smile. "This whole conversation is crazy. And yet so real. Have I really only known you a day?" He kissed her and helped her back into her seat. When she was buckled into her seatbelt again, he shifted into drive. "Are we still going to the casino?" He glanced her way, catching her nod.

"We are," she said.

He sighed. "We're going to need an army to resolve this situation."

"I was hoping you might know where we can get one."

"Maybe not an army, but Hank Patterson knows people. I'm hoping he has an idea what to do."

"In the meantime, I want to confront Trevor Spotted Elk in a public setting like Wanda suggested." She held out her hand.

Carter took it in his. "I'm hoping that, surrounded by other people, he won't try anything stupid."

"Me, too." She squeezed his hand.

Carter braced himself for the meeting, praying Trevor wouldn't be there, thus putting off what would eventually have to happen. Amanda wasn't going to back down. If Trevor was responsible for the deaths of the teens and the attack on Joe, the asshole would know Amanda's fury.

CHAPTER 10

AMANDA SAT BESIDE CARTER, her hand in his, feeling stunned, elated and scared all at once.

One day.

And one amazing night making love.

It was infatuation. That's all there was to it. People didn't fall in love that fast.

She cast a shy glance his way.

The man wasn't the most handsome man she'd ever seen.

Oh, who was she kidding? His broad shoulders, six-pack abs and toned muscles were positively delicious.

Why would he be interested in her? She was just… Amanda, a mixed breed who looked much like the other women on the reservation, except for her blue eyes… the only thing she had inherited from her white mother.

She liked him. A lot. Was that enough? Was it love? She'd never really been in love. Yeah, she'd dated in high school and college, but nothing that had lasted. There hadn't been enough of a spark to keep a flame burning.

Now, with Carter…there were sparks enough to light a forest fire. Was it enough to last? Should she take her own advice and live in the present, love while she could and stock up on memories?

Hell, yes. Even if the present didn't last very long. Whoever was behind all the murders and attacks was dangerous and not afraid to kill. Their days could be numbered.

Her hand tightened around Carter's. Could she stand losing someone she loved? The only person she'd ever really loved was Joe. He'd saved her from the foster system and had been the father she'd always wanted. The thought of losing him made her heart squeeze hard in her chest. Seeing him lying in the hospital bed, battered and nearly beaten to death, had been heartbreaking.

But she was forever grateful for having been a part of his life and would do it all over again, even knowing she might lose him. She'd been afraid to love when Joe had taken her in. Her own family had abandoned her. The foster families had never loved her.

Amanda had been certain she would never know

what love was...until Joe had taken her home and treated her like a daughter should be treated.

When he'd been mad at her, he hadn't hit her. He hadn't belittled her or given her back to the foster system. He'd stood by her and helped her navigate the remainder of high school when she'd been behind and had to catch up. He'd helped her enroll in college, bought her books and paid her living expenses until she'd graduated.

They'd spent their holidays together, celebrating Thanksgiving and Christmas, just the two of them. He was family, and he'd taught her what uncondi-tional love was.

Could she love someone else? Was she willing to try? Was that someone Carter?

Her heart swelled inside her chest at the same time as butterflies filled her belly. A one-night stand was easy. No commitment. No false promises. No messy feelings.

Falling in love?

Whoa.

Her stomach roiled, and her heart beat faster. She was scared. No, terrified. And strangely hopeful.

And they were in the middle of a potential gang war that had a very uncertain outcome.

Was it worth the risk to let herself fall in love?

She drew in a lungful of air and let it out slowly. With that steadying breath, a rush of well-being filled her.

Why not let whatever was going to happen happen?

If it was love, great. If it wasn't meant to be, at least she wouldn't regret not giving them a chance.

All the crazy thoughts went through her head as they drove to the casino.

Carter was silent beside her.

Amanda wondered if he had the same ideas going through his head as she had going through hers. She couldn't tell just by looking at him.

As they neared the casino, she pulled her attention back to what was even more immediate and important.

Carter parked the truck as close to the entrance as possible, got out and hurried around to help Amanda down.

She waited for him, wanting to feel his hands on her body, so reassuring in their firmness.

For a moment, she stood on the ground in his embrace, girding her loins for the encounter with Trevor.

"Let's start this by looking like any other gamblers," Carter said into her ear. "We go in and have a look around before we start asking about Trevor. Are you okay with that?"

She nodded, looked up into his eyes and smiled. "Thank you. You ground me."

He gave her a tight smile, kissed her briefly and drew her hand through the crook of his arm.

"What's your favorite? Poker, roulette, craps or slots?"

"I've never actually gambled in a casino. I've been here a couple of times to talk to parents of some of the teens I work with, but never to play. I do know how to play poker. I earned some spending money playing in college."

Carter grinned. "I like you more and more each day. A good mix of virtue and vice. Come on. Let's see how good your poker face is." He walked with her into the casino.

Like she'd told him, she'd been inside the casino on a few occasions. The constant pinging of bells and whirling sounds made by the slot machines filled the air like a cheap carnival. Many of the patrons were older, gray or white-haired, some with their walkers, others smoking cigarettes, parked in front of slot machines, pulling the handle or pressing the spin button—the cylinder in front of them spinning, spinning, spinning, before finally coming to a stop.

Each person hoped to win a jackpot and go home a millionaire. Most went home hundreds or thousands of dollars poorer.

Waitresses moved among the guests, offering drinks. Perhaps the drinks numbed their senses and made them spend more before they finally gave up and went back to their rooms for the night or, in many cases, in the early morning hours.

Amanda's gaze panned the room, searching for anyone looking like security staff.

Considering it was still daytime, the crowd was thin, and staffing was thinner. Only a couple of the blackjack tables were open, one roulette wheel and a table for poker. The rest stood empty, waiting for the afternoon and evening patronage.

"Think we're here too early?" Amanda whispered.

"Maybe. I see a man in a suit ahead. Perhaps he's the manager."

Amanda's gaze found the suit. "Yes, of course. That's Theo Nighthawk. He's the manager. I've seen him at some of the local events and job fairs. The casino sponsors sports leagues and local events. They give a lot of money to the annual pow wow and host cultural dancing events at the casino once a week during the summer tourist season."

"He's coming this way," Carter said.

Amanda pasted a smile on her face as the casino manager approached them.

"Mr. Nighhawk." Amanda held out her hand. "I don't think we've formally met. I'm Amanda Small."

"Ms. Small, my pleasure." The casino manager took her hand in a loose handshake that could barely be registered in firmness. "You're the new counselor in Fort Washakie, aren't you?"

"Not so new, but yes." Amanda pulled back her hand and turned to Carter. "This is my fiancé, Carter Manning."

The casino manager met Carter's gaze. "Congratulations on your engagement." His gaze raked Carter from head to toe. "Tell me, Mr. Manning, are you a descendent of a Native American?"

Carter shook his head. "Not that I know of, Mr. Nighthawk. My family is out of Texas. I haven't taken the time to explore our genealogy." He slipped his arm around Amanda's back and pulled her close. "Amanda is as close as I get."

Nighthawk's eyes narrowed for a second, and then his brow smoothed. "You must call me Theo. Mr. Nighthawk is far too formal for our playground."

Carter tipped his head. "Theo."

Amanda looked around the casino. "Business is good?"

The casino manager shrugged. "Not as good as in past years. Many of our regulars have either died off or are confined to nursing homes and can't make the trip out to our casino anymore."

Amanda cringed at the thought of older people spending their hard-earned retirement money gambling. Like any addiction, it was a tough one to quit.

"Is there anything I can help you with while you're here?" Theo asked.

"As a matter of fact, I had hoped to talk with one of your employees, Trever Spotted Elk. Is he here today?" Amanda asked with a smile.

"I'm not certain; let me ask." Theo Nighthawk

turned to a wiry man with short black hair and brown eyes, sweeping up discarded candy wrappers and empty cups and cans. "Eddie, is Mr. Spotted Elk currently in the building?"

The man he'd addressed as Eddie nodded. "Yes, sir. Would you like me to get him?"

"Yes, please," Theo said.

"Trevor!" Eddie called out.

Theo shook his head. "My apologies," he said to Amanda and glared at Eddie. "Go find Mr. Spotted Elk."

For a moment, Eddie hesitated, appearing as if he wanted to argue with the casino manager. He opened his mouth and closed it without uttering a word. Then he spun on his heel and hurried away.

"It's hard to get good help." Theo's frowning gaze followed Eddie. "I can barely get enough staff to wait on the people on the patio who brave the late summer heat for a meal. But that isn't your issue, is it?"

"No, sir," Amanda said. "I'm here to prove to my fiancé, who is not afraid of horses like me, that there is so much more to do on the reservation than ride."

"I'm sure he will find this place entertaining. After you're married, are you going to leave us for a bigger city, or stay and work with the youth?"

"I'm planning on staying and working with the teens as I am now."

Theo cocked an eyebrow. "And Mr. Manning? I'm

afraid there aren't nearly as many jobs as people on the rez. What will you do while your wife works with the young people?"

Carter gave the man a hint of a smile. "I have a job. I work remotely. Don't worry. I'm not going to take any jobs away from the people of the reservation."

Theo dipped his head. "That's good to hear." His gaze went past Carter. "Ahh, there's Mr. Spotted Elk now."

Carter and Amanda turned.

Eddie kept pace with another man with tattooed arms, high cheekbones and long dark hair pulled back into a neat ponytail. He wore a black, security guard uniform and carried a radio clipped to his shoulder.

The man with the ponytail gave Amanda and Carter a narrow-eyed glare. "What do you want?"

"Could we have a moment of your time in private?" Amanda did her best to flash the semblance of a smile. A very tight one.

"I'm a busy man," Trevor said.

Amanda's eyes narrowed to match his. "I imagine you are, with one full-time job and another that I'm sure takes more of your time."

Trevor's eyes narrowed into slits. "I don't know what you're talking about."

"The Wind River Police Chief is lying in the Riverton Hospital in the ICU—which I'm sure you already knew." Anger flared, and Amanda dropped all pretenses of civility. She advanced on Trevor. "Joe Sharp Spear is a good man, looking out for the good of the reservation. He's dedicated his life to helping others. He did not deserve what you and your gang did to him." She poked a finger at Trevor's chest. "And don't get me started on the teens you are so callously murdering."

Trevor grabbed her wrist and held it. "Stop now," he said, his tone low and menacing.

"Or what? You'll push me off a cliff or bridge or drown me in a lake? Or are you going to do like you did to Joe and beat me with a baseball bat or tire iron to get your message across?" She stood toe to toe with the man, six inches shorter but no less intimidating in her fury.

At least, she hoped so.

"Let go of her wrist," Carter said to Trevor.

"I'll let go when I'm good and ready," Trevor said with a growl in his tone.

"You'll let go now." Carter stepped forward, his fists raised, his jaw hard.

"She picked this fight, not me," Trevor said. "I didn't ask to be attacked at work. Take your woman and get the hell out of this casino."

"Whoa," the casino manager held up his hands. "Let's not get into a pissing contest." He glanced around as if assessing whether their interaction was garnering attention from the patrons. "Perhaps you should take this conversation outside." He moved toward Amanda and Trevor, his arms held out as if herding sheep.

The man named Eddie stepped up beside Nighthawk, his face poker straight. "Yes, please, take it outside."

Trevor released Amanda's wrist. "I have nothing to say to this woman. I don't know what she's talking about."

Carter grabbed Amanda around the waist and held her back from launching herself at Trevor. "Come on, darling, let's take it outside."

"You can take *her* outside," Trevor said. "I'm not going. I haven't done anything to Joe or those teenagers. You've got the wrong guy."

"You're the leader of the NA Syndicate, are you not?" Amanda demanded.

Trevor lifted his chin. "I am."

"And you're saying you had nothing to do with the deaths of the teens and the attack on Joe?" Amanda frowned. "You're lying!"

Trevor shrugged. "Believe what you will."

"You were at Tara Running Fox's home earlier today, threatening her family," Amanda said. "You can't say you weren't. She saw you."

He looked down his nose at her. "You can't prove that. It would be her word against mine, and it's on the rez. Nobody cares."

"Where were you early this morning when my

house was attacked and my fiancé's truck was tagged?" Amanda asked. "It had to be you and the NA Syndicate."

"I was home in my bed," Trevor said, "ask my girlfriend."

Amanda's eyes narrowed. The man had to be lying. "If not the NA Syndicate, then who?"

Trevor's pupils flared for a second, and then his face returned to poker straight. "I can't say. I wasn't there."

"Can't or won't?" Amanda was so tired of all the secrecy.

"I've told you everything I know." He nodded toward Nighthawk. "I'll get back to work now."

"Thank you, Trevor," Nighthawk said.

Trevor spun on his heel and walked away, his head held high.

Amanda leaned back against Carter. "I don't understand how he can get away with what he's done."

"Unless you have proof, you have nothing on my employee." Nighthawk nodded toward Eddie, his face stern. "If that's all you needed from us, I have a ride to catch in a helicopter. Mr. Black Bear will escort you to the exit. It can be confusing finding your way out of the casino. We wouldn't want you to get lost."

In other words, Nighthawk wanted Amanda and Carter out of his casino before they disturbed anyone else.

Amanda dipped her head and bit out, "Thank you for your time."

Nighthawk leaned close to Eddie and whispered something only Eddie could hear.

Eddie nodded.

The casino manager left them standing there and disappeared among the slot machines.

Disappointed, Amanda allowed Carter to loop her hand through the crook of his arm and walk with her behind Eddie, who led them by the most direct route to the front entrance.

Eddie stepped outside the casino with them and stopped just outside the range of the automated door's sensor. "Mr. Nighthawk would like you to make an appointment next time you come to the casino to accuse one of his staff members of murder or assault."

Amanda scowled at the man. "Tell Mr. Nighthawk—"

"Tell him 'thank you' for his time," Carter concluded.

The whomping of rotor blades beating the air made all three glance up. A helicopter lifted off the casino roof, circled once and then headed north.

"When did the casino get a helicopter?" Amanda asked.

Eddie shook his head. "It's not the casino's. It belongs to a friend of Mr. Nighthawk's." The man spun and reentered the casino without looking back.

Carter took Amanda's hand and led her away from the casino and back to his damaged truck.

Amanda didn't want to leave. Deep down, she knew that whoever was responsible for the teens' deaths and Joe's attack had to be nearby. Her gut told her the killer or the one calling the shots was inside that casino.

She sat in the truck, fighting the urge to march back inside and demand to see a complete list of names of the staff.

The killer was in there. He had to be.

When Carter took his seat behind the steering wheel, Amanda looked over at him. "Do you ever get strong twinges of instinct that you just know is absolutely correct?"

Carter nodded. "I usually act on those instead of standing back and letting them pass. Even if my gut is wrong, I'd rather stop something from happening and take the heat if I'm wrong than not stop it and regret it later. Why? What is your gut telling you?"

She drew in a deep breath and stared at the casino. "My gut tells me the killer is inside the casino."

"Do you want to go back inside and question anyone else?" Carter asked.

Amanda shook her head. "No. I wouldn't know where to start, and everyone is pretty tight-lipped."

"They might have good reason to be so secretive. Tara was hesitant to tell you anything. Maybe they've all been threatened with death if they reveal anything about what's going on."

Amanda's lips pinched together. "There has to be a weak link. Someone has to be willing to talk."

"Where to?" Carter pulled out of the casino parking lot and headed back toward Fort Washakie.

"I'd like to make sure Tara and her family are getting relocated safely," she said.

"We can do that with a phone call to Stone," Carter suggested.

"I'd like to see for myself." She gave him a crooked smile. "Not that I don't trust your friend. I'm worried they won't make it off the reservation alive. I believe Tara when she said she recognized Trevor. Now that he knows we're onto him, he might take his threats to the next level."

Carter tipped his head, his brow furrowing. "He seemed convincing when he said he had nothing to do with the deaths of the teens and the attack on Joe."

"He has to be lying, and I'm afraid for Tara and her family."

"Check and see if they're still there," Carter said.

Amanda called Tara's number. It rang five times with no answer and went to her voicemail. Knowing reception was sketchy at best on the reservation, Amanda called again, not expecting an answer.

On the second ring, Tara's voice said, "Amanda, I'm glad you called. I wanted to thank you and your fiancé for helping get my family off the reservation. They left twenty minutes ago with Stone and Kyla."

Amanda gripped the cell phone tighter, her heart sinking to the pit of her belly. "Wait. What do you mean *they* left? Aren't you with them?"

"I'm sorry. I know you wanted me to go with them, but I couldn't. Not when my other family is still at risk. The Young Wolves need me, and I can't desert them. Keme and the others are in danger. If I leave, that puts them at more risk. Those who have their grip on us warned us that if anyone tries to leave, they will punish those left behind. So, you see, I couldn't leave. I couldn't live with myself if one of my Young Wolves bore the brunt of my cowardice."

"Tara, it's not cowardice," Amanda argued. "Your mother and younger siblings need you, too. Going with them would've been the brave thing to do."

"I'm going to tell you something I'm not supposed to tell anyone. I don't expect you to do anything, but if I don't make it back, I want you to let my mother, brother and sister know that I love them and that Tobi and I did what we did so that they would have a better life. That's all the Young Wolves wanted was to help our families live a better life."

"Tara, you need to tell them yourself. If it's that dangerous, you don't need to go."

Carter pulled the truck to the side of the road and waited while Amanda spoke to the teen.

"It's happening whether I'm there or not.

However, I will be there—Saturday at midnight at the bluffs near Alkali Lake. Shit's going down. It's going to be big, and the ones in charge will be heavily armed. I will be there for my Wolves."

"Tara, please," Amanda begged. "I need more information if I'm to help in any way."

"You can't," the teen said. "It's too big and involves people on the rez and off. Anyone who tries to stop it will be killed. Anyone who fails to show will be killed or their families targeted. The Young Wolves wanted out. Unfortunately, someone got word that we were considering getting out before we got too deep. It was already too late. The three who've died were a message to the rest."

"Please, Tara," Amanda said.

Carter gripped her hand, pulled her cell phone close and punched the speaker button. "Tara, Carter here. We want to help. Can you at least give us a clue as to who you're dealing with?"

"I've already said too much." Her voice caught on a sob. "If they have a way of listening, I'm dead. I'm pretty sure that's what happened to Tobi, Allison and Ryan. Those in charge wanted to send a message. I'm probably setting them up for more retribution by telling you anything. I know you're trying to help. You deserved to know. I'm going to disappear until Saturday. Don't try to find Keme or me. We've started down this path. We have no option but to see it to the end."

CHAPTER 11

"Saturday." Carter shook his head. "That's only two days away. Two days to figure out what's going down."

"Two days to stop further carnage." Amanda stared at the cell phone in her hand. "I can't begin to imagine what Tara and her friends have gotten themselves into."

"Well, we have a timeframe and a potential location. That's more than we had before." He pulled out his cell phone and called Stone.

"Carter," Stone answered. "Might not have reception for long. We're well on our way to West Yellowstone with the Running Fox family. Tara refused to come with us. I texted that information to you, but it might not have gone through."

"It didn't. However, we did get a call from Tara letting us know she hadn't gone with her family. She also told us something big is going down on Saturday at the bluffs at Alkali Lake. She couldn't say what and was scared about telling us that much. If we're going to help, we'll need more than just our team at West Yellowstone."

"Understood," Stone said. "You have Hank's number. Call him while you have good cell phone reception and fill him in on what you know. He'll know what to do and who to involve. And, Carter, you can count on our team for sure. I'll get them ready to mobilize and start your way as soon as possible. Two days isn't much to prepare."

"We've handled worse on shorter notice," Carter reminded him.

Stone chuckled. "Yes, we have. We survived as a team. Don't try to do it alone."

"Roger. I'll call Hank. Out here," he said and ended the call. The next call was to Hank Patterson, the former Navy SEAL who'd started the Brotherhood Protectors in Eagle Rock, Montana, engaging former special operations, highly trained operatives to fulfill whatever needs they deemed necessary.

Carter hoped Saturday's needs weren't out of the scope of what the Brotherhood Protectors could manage.

He called Hank.

The man picked up on the first ring. "Carter Manning, I understand things are heating up on Wind River Reservation."

"Yes, sir." Carter filled him in on all that had happened since he'd arrived on the reservation and what Tara had said about an event on Saturday. "I wish we had more information, but we don't. Tara said Saturday would be big. We have no idea what 'big' entails. Any additional help we can get would be appreciated."

"I'm betting since they have an undercover DEA on the reservation, it's drug-related," Hank said. "I'll put out feelers with the DEA, Department of Homeland Security and anyone else who might help."

"We haven't located the DEA agent."

"You know, if you discover who it is, to protect him, it's probably better if you don't engage with him," Hank said. "We'll work it from the other end as if we don't know there's someone there. I'll get to work and see who we can muster and if they have any further information on what might be headed to Wind River."

"Thanks," Carter said. "Any help is better than nothing."

"If we can't get other agencies involved, you can count on our teams in Montana and Colorado. And, of course, your team in Yellowstone." Hank ended the call.

Carter glanced across at Amanda. "Let's hope two days is enough to mobilize the army we might need to handle the something big coming this way on Saturday."

Amanda shook her head. "In the meantime, we have to stay alive until that date and time. That gives us two days to continue our own search for answers."

Carter held out his hand.

Amanda placed hers in his. "You're not going to try to talk me out of finding out more, despite the danger?"

He shook his head. "No. I'm learning it does no good to caution you. The best I can do is to be there to block the bullets."

Amanda frowned. "I'm flattered that you would take a bullet for me, but I don't want you to die because I was reckless."

"Then don't be reckless," he said with a smile. Carter leaned across and pressed a kiss to her lips. "I'd really like to spend more time with you that doesn't involve people threatening our lives. It would be nice to have a regular date to see if we're compatible when we're not under extreme stress."

Amanda grinned. "We could turn out to be pretty darned boring."

Carter's lips twisted into a wry grin. "Boring would be nice about now."

She nodded, her smile fading. "I admit, I'm worried about Saturday. If this is drug-related, who else is involved? I've read the reports. The Mexican cartels target reservations. Our people are vulnerable with unemployment so high and many of our people already abusing alcohol. Getting them addicted to hard-core drugs like meth, cocaine, and whatever else, is all too easy."

"Not to mention the money that can be made selling the stuff," Carter reminded her.

"Tara said they'd gotten into whatever they're into because they'd wanted their families to have better lives." Amanda's lips pressed together. "Sounds to me like the promise of riches."

"And she said the Young Wolves didn't do the drugs, even though the first two who died had meth in their systems." Carter's eyes narrowed. "We should check with the ME about Tobi's lab results."

"I'm betting on the meth," Amanda said. "Those kids probably thought they could deal drugs and provide for their families."

"They didn't take into account the drug dealers are playing for keeps," Carter said. "Once they have you, they don't let go."

"If something big is happening on Saturday, it's probably a shipment arriving," Amanda said.

Carter nodded. "All hands will be on deck to receive and distribute. A lot of product and money will be involved."

"You'd think the DEA would've gotten wind of something that big."

"I'm sure shipments go undetected all the time." Carter shifted his truck into Drive and pulled out onto the highway. "Where to now?"

"I thought we might visit some of the other

members of the Young Wolves and see if they'll share any more information than Tara already has."

"Starting with?" Carter prompted.

"KC Sun Dancer." Amanda gave him directions to KC's home on the other side of Fort Washakie.

"Who is he?"

"She," Amanda corrected. "From previous conversations with Tara, KC and Tara grew up together. They are best friends, and KC was Tobi's girlfriend."

"As his girlfriend, KC might have been the last one to text or call him before his death," Carter said.

"I was thinking the same." Amanda smiled at Carter. "I like the way we think alike."

"Do you think she'll be like Tara and hide until Saturday?" Carter asked.

"It's possible." Amanda frowned. "Or she could be hiding in plain sight. She's a part-time waitress at a diner in Riverton."

"Good. We can get something to eat and interview her at the same time."

Amanda's belly rumbled. "I didn't even realize I was hungry until the mention of eating. Now, I'm starved."

Carter glanced at his watch. "We've missed breakfast and lunch. We can have dinner."

"Sounds great. I'd offer to cook dinner," Amanda snorted softly, "but I don't think it's a good idea to go back to my place."

"Definitely not," Carter agreed.

"It's just as well; my refrigerator is pretty much empty except for maybe a jar of pickles and some condiments." She grimaced. "I meant to get groceries yesterday but went to West Yellowstone instead."

"I'm glad you did," Carter said. "I can't imagine you wading through what's happened on your own."

"While we're in Riverton, I'd like to run by the hospital and check on Joe." Amanda stared out the front windshield. "Hopefully, he will have come to and can identify his attackers."

"We can do that. We might consider staying at a hotel in Riverton since your cottage is out of the question."

Amanda nodded. "Good idea. It's a bigger town. We can hope the NA Syndicate won't be bold enough to come after us there."

As they pulled into Riverton, the sun was well on its way toward the western horizon, creating a dazzling display, and reminding Carter that while humans struggled with the day-to-day issues of being human, nature continued, business as usual.

"By the time we finish at the diner, it'll be getting too late to do much else," Carter noted.

Amanda nodded. "If we don't get much out of KC, we can look for Josh Tall Grass, Nina Sweetwater or Dylan Many Paths tomorrow morning."

Carter followed Amanda's directions to the diner and parked near the door.

"I see KC through the windows," Amanda said. "Come on. Let's see if she'll be more forthcoming."

Before Carter could get around to open Amanda's door, she was on the ground and joining him at the front of the truck.

Carter held the diner door open. Amanda entered and found a table at the far side of the room where the waitress she'd indicated was working the tables.

KC was a young teen with long dark hair, wearing a T-shirt with the diner logo splashed across the front. She stopped at their table and smiled at Amanda. "Hi, Amanda. Is this the fiancé everyone is talking about?"

Amanda nodded. "Good to see you, KC. Yes, this is Carter, my fiancé."

Carter liked how easily his name rolled off her tongue, along with being called her fiancé. The old saying, *fake it until you feel it,* struck him suddenly. Was that what was happening? They'd told everyone they'd met they were engaged. It had already become natural to hear her refer to him as her fiancé and for him to introduce her as such.

For someone who'd sworn off ever marrying or falling in love again, Carter had fully embraced the fake engagement. And what bothered him was that it didn't bother him.

"Congratulations," KC said. "You're getting a nice woman for your wife. Amanda has been there for us."

KC met Amanda's gaze and whispered, "Thank you for what you did for the Running Foxes."

Amanda acknowledged her with a simple nod.

"What would you like to drink," KC asked more loudly.

Carter ordered coffee, his first for the day, and he needed it. Even though it was getting late, he might need the caffeine boost. He wasn't sure they'd be safe in Riverton. Staying awake might be an option to ensure their safety.

"I'll have water," Amanda said.

KC left and returned with their drinks and asked what they wanted to eat.

"I'll have the meatloaf, green beans and roasted potatoes." Carter closed the menu and looked at Amanda.

"I'll have the same," she said with a smile and handed over her menu. "KC, when you get a minute, can we talk?"

The teen's ready smile slipped. "I'm really busy," she said, glancing around the nearly empty diner, her dark cheeks filling with a dusty red tone.

Amanda reached out and touched KC's arm. "I'm worried about you and the others."

KC's gaze darted around the diner and through the large windows to the street and sidewalks beyond. "It's not a good idea."

Just like Amanda had pointed out, the windows

were large and allowed people passing by the diner to look in and see who was there.

If the NA Syndicate was keeping the Young Wolves under surveillance, the diner would be too exposed to allow them to carry on a conversation unnoticed.

Amanda nodded. "Can you tell me where the ladies' room is?"

KC's gaze connected with Amanda's, and she gave an almost imperceptible nod.

"Back right corner. There's a short hallway. You'll find the ladies' room there." KC held up their order. "I'll get your food ordered."

KC left their table and passed their order through to the kitchen.

Amanda found her way to the short hallway at the back of the diner and entered the ladies' room.

She squirted soap into her hands and turned on the water.

A moment later, KC entered the bathroom with a quick glance back over her shoulder.

"I'm sorry, but I think we're all being watched," KC said.

"Amanda continued to wash her hands. "By whom?"

"The NA Syndicate and the other gang." KC's brow furrowed. "We all want out, but we can't leave," she whispered. She took Amanda's hands. "I'm scared."

Amanda pulled her into her arms for a brief hug and then stepped away. "I can't promise anything, but we'll try to help. Can you tell me the names of the people you're most scared of?"

KC shook her head. "Tobi tried to get word off the rez about what was going on. You know what that got him."

"Did he text you about what he planned?"

She nodded. "I deleted them, and he said he deleted his as well."

"What did he say?" Amanda asked.

A woman pushed through the door at that moment and hurried to one of the stalls.

KC and Amanda went through the motions of washing their hands very slowly.

What felt like hours later, the woman in the stall flushed and came out to wash her hands. She smiled briefly as she dried her hands with a paper towel and left the room.

"Tobi said he was going to talk to the Feds." KC shook her head. "I don't know where he was meeting or who exactly he met with. He didn't say." The girl swallowed hard. "The last thing he texted was, *I'm going to get help. I love you.*" KC's eyes flooded. She tore off a paper towel and dabbed at the moisture. "I guess he never made it to that meeting. Instead, he ended up at the bottom of a cliff." She bit down on her lip.

"What are the Young Wolves involved in that has you so scared?"

She looked away. "I can't."

"If you want help, you have to trust someone."

KC's brow twisted. "The trouble is, we don't know who to trust. They're everywhere and always watching. For all I know, that woman who just came into the bathroom could be one of them. They mean it when they tell you to keep their secrets. If you don't, you die." She ducked her head. "Like Allison, Ryan and Tobi. I can't die. The money I make goes to my mother and little brother. It's not much, but it helps keep the lights on."

"KC, we can't help you if we don't know who or what we're up against." Amanda captured her gaze. "You mentioned another gang? Besides the NA Syndicate?"

She looked over her shoulder before nodding. "They're even worse than the Syndicate. They call themselves the Arapaho Lords or Lords, for short. They were part of the NA Syndicate. At least a dozen broke off recently to form their own gang. Some say their leader is just a puppet for someone who is pulling his strings. No one knows who it is, but the puppet is Colt Kickingwoman."

KC looked back over her shoulder. "I have to get back to work before anyone comes looking for me."

"Will you be safe getting home? Hell, will you be safe at home?"

KC nodded. "I live behind the police station in

Fort Washakie. I'll leave here in a few minutes and go straight home."

Amanda gave the young woman her card with her personal cell phone number on the back. "Call me if you need help or want to share anything else."

KC pocketed the card and slipped out of the bathroom.

Amanda waited a minute longer, then left the ladies' room and resumed her seat across from Carter.

"Everything okay?" he asked quietly.

Amanda smiled. "Yes. Piece by piece, we might get the whole picture," she said so softly only he could hear.

KC reappeared a moment later with two plates of food. "Enjoy," she said. "And thank you."

The meal was amazing. Amanda was so full when she was finished, she groaned. "I won't need to eat until tomorrow night."

Carter paid the bill and escorted her out the door.

The sun had settled below the horizon with the last bit of light, a gray haze making everything shadowy.

Amanda strained to see into the shadows. After the previous night and what had happened to Joe, she was super vigilant, watching for anyone who might jump out and harm them.

Without being reminded, Carter drove her to the

Riverton Hospital, where they rode the elevator up to the ICU floor.

Joe lay as they'd left him earlier. A nurse was in his room checking his vital signs.

Amanda crossed to the opposite side of the hospital bed from the nurse and took Joe's hand in hers. "Any change?"

The nurse shook her head. "None. Though his heart is beating strong. We all hope he comes out of it soon. He's loved by so many on the reservation."

"Has a member of hospital security been stationed outside his door all day?" Carter asked.

The nurse nodded. "Yes, he has. He says there will be another man coming on duty soon."

Amanda sighed. "Good. We still don't know for certain who did this to him."

"We're keeping a close eye on Mr. Sharp Spear," the nurse said. "If you need anything while you're here, let me know."

"Thank you for all you're doing for Joe," Amanda said.

The nurse's lips twisted. "I wish we could do more. Time is what he needs. Time to heal." She left Amanda and Carter in the room with Joe.

Amanda leaned over the bed and pressed a kiss to Joe's cheek. It was warm, which was comforting. Now, if only he would open his eyes and look up at her, asking her why she wasn't working, she'd be so relieved.

She waited there for thirty minutes with no change, all the while speaking to him. "Joe, we need you to wake up, even if it's only for a minute or two. Please, wake up."

"We need to secure a room for the night," Carter said.

She nodded. "I'm tired to the bone."

They left, and Carter drove to the nearest reputable hotel and parked.

"This is going to look weird with no luggage," Amanda noted. "I'm too tired to care."

"Remember, we're engaged," he said.

She nodded.

At the front desk, Carter asked for a room, toothbrushes and toothpaste.

She could survive on a full stomach and clean teeth. Tomorrow, they would swing by her house and shower in the daylight. Assuming it was still standing and not burned to the ground.

Amanda didn't even balk at sharing a room with Carter. After the previous night, she looked forward to being with him, making love and sleeping beside him. He made her feel so good in so many ways. She was getting used to having him around.

They didn't say much as they entered the room on the second floor, closed the door and automatically began stripping out of their clothes, the garments dropping so fast they left them where they landed.

Carter took her hand and led her into the shower,

where they took their time washing every inch of the other's body until they were so hot that Carter turned off the water, grabbed towels, and they hurriedly dried.

Then he carried Amanda into the bedroom and made love to her into the night.

She fell asleep in his arms, replete and as happy as she could be with the pending deadline of *something big happening Saturday night at the bluffs at Alkali Lake.*

CHAPTER 12

CARTER WOKE with Amanda lying beside him, her body warm against his. He remained still, drinking in everything about her, from her silky, thick hair to her smooth dark skin pressed against his.

No rocks came flying through the windows, just sunshine sneaking around the edges of the blackout curtains. He couldn't help thinking this is what it could be like every morning if he opened his heart completely and let himself love again.

The looming Saturday meeting had him tied in knots. Somehow, he had to convince Amanda to let the Brotherhood Protectors handle it. The fact Tara had mentioned the people at the location would be heavily armed had been the deciding factor.

The Brotherhood Protectors were all former special operations. They knew what to do and how to enter a hot zone. What they had to keep in mind was that there would be teenagers there who didn't want to be but had been compelled by threats to their teammates and their families.

And the fact the meeting location was on a reservation made it even more complicated. The feds had to be invited in by the tribe. Hank might have friends in the DEA and Homeland Security, but they couldn't trespass on Indian lands without explicit permission.

The Brotherhood Protectors didn't work for the US government anymore. They were civilians now. From what he'd learned about Hank and his team of warriors, they didn't always play by the rules. Swede's ability to hack into any computer system was a case in point. The Brotherhood worked cases local, state and federal law enforcement might not be able to touch.

They wouldn't let a line on a map stop them from going where they needed to be.

"Hey." Amanda's eyes blinked open, and she looked up into his. "Is it already morning?"

He nodded. "We actually slept in. It's almost nine o'clock."

She rolled onto her side and touched his chest with the tips of her fingers. "Checkout isn't until eleven..." Amanda's lips curled as she traced a line around one of his little brown nipples and then moved down over his ribs and belly. Her hand circled his full erection and tugged gently. "I was going to ask if you were up for some morning exercise." She grinned. "I'm assuming this is a yes."

He laughed and kissed her hard. "We have today and tomorrow to figure out everything we can. I feel like we're already running out of time and should be up and running." Despite his words, his hands slid leisurely over her shoulder, down to her waist and across her rounded hip. He pulled her closer until his cock nudged her belly. "We can postpone the start of the day for a little longer."

"Mmm. Good. I was thinking I'd have to convince you to stay in bed."

"Oh, sweetheart, I'm fully convinced and ready to rock."

Her lips spread wider in a seductive smile. In a swift move, she rolled him onto his back and straddled his hips. "Got any more protection?"

He tipped his head toward the nightstand. "In the drawer."

She leaned over and reached into the drawer, extracting a single packet and setting it on the pillow beside Carter's head.

He frowned. "Are we going to need that?"

Amanda nodded. "But first…" She scooted down his legs, wrapped her hands around his shaft and leaned down to touch her tongue to the tip.

He leaned his head back against the pillow and moaned. "I like how you set your priorities."

"All work and no play…and all that," she

murmured and then slid her tongue around the rim while gently using her hands to massage lower down.

He caught his breath, the sensations so intense he was afraid he wouldn't last long enough to satisfy her. Focusing on control, he lay still, allowing her to do what she was doing.

She took him into her mouth and sucked gently.

It felt so good he raised his hips, sinking deeper until he bumped into the back of her throat.

Amanda drew back until he was almost all the way out and then sank again. She repeated the actions, again and again, fondling him as she worked magic with her mouth.

He dug his fingers into her thick hair and thrust upward, setting the pace and increasing it with the buildup of tension in his body.

As he neared the edge, it took all of his control to pull free and hold his release long enough to flip her onto her belly and raise her hips.

Carter entered her from behind, sliding into her tight channel aided by her warm, slick juices.

Once he was fully sheathed, he remained there long enough for her to adjust to his girth. Holding tightly to his control, he pulled free, grabbed the condom on the pillow, ripped it open and rolled it down over his throbbing shaft.

"I'm glad someone is thinking," she murmured into the pillow. Her fingers curled into the comforter as he eased into her again. Holding her hips firmly in his hands, he thrust into her again and again, moving faster and harder.

She rose on her hands and rocked backward, matching his rhythm, her back arching as she reached her climax.

He came soon after in an explosion of his senses that radiated throughout his body. He buried himself inside her and bent over her back to cup her breasts in his palms. He rode the waves of his release all the way to the end.

Then he pulled free, eased Amanda down onto the mattress and rolled her onto her back. "You are amazing."

She smiled up at him. "Ditto."

He laid beside her and gathered her into his arms. "We're going to make it through this," he murmured against her neck.

"Yes, we are. I want more of this," she said. "More of you."

"And I can't get enough of you." His arms tightened around her. For a long time, he held on, not wanting the moment to end.

The sounds of the housekeeping staff rolling carts in the hallway shattered the bubble of their oasis.

Amanda sighed. "It's time."

He nodded and rolled out of bed onto his feet.

She reached out a hand, and he helped her up.

Together, they walked into the bathroom and rinsed off in the shower, kissing and touching until the water grew cold.

A few minutes later, they were dried off and dressed in the clothes they'd worn the day before. They headed out to start their day of searching for more clues to better prepare them for what was coming on Saturday.

No matter how the day ended, the start was theirs to remember and cherish.

Carter chose to cherish any memory he could make with this remarkable woman who cared enough about others she put her own life in the line of fire. He hoped he was enough to protect her. If not, he prayed that Hank would come through with back up in time to keep her alive. Life on the reservation was hard with so many strikes against the young people. They needed Amanda to help them navigate the pitfalls and the triumphs.

"I'd like to stop by my house to change into fresh clothes," Amanda said.

"I was going to suggest the same. I left my duffel bag there."

They accomplished the drive from Riverton to Fort Washakie in record time. As he pulled up to the cottage Amanda had called home, he shook his head. The red paint was garish. The broken windows and the door standing open made the little house look abandoned.

"I liked this little house," Amanda said. "It always looked happy to me. Now…it's sad." She frowned as she dropped down from the truck and joined Carter at the base of the steps leading up to the porch. "I don't remember leaving the door open."

Alarm bells and red flags went up in Carter's mind. "Go back to the truck," he said, his tone hard, brooking no argument.

She backed away, her brow knitting. "Do you think someone might still be inside?"

"I don't know, but I'd feel a whole lot better if you got into the truck, locked the door and ducked below the dash."

The tone of his voice must have registered with her. Amanda did as she was told. Carter waited until she was inside the truck and ducking low before he moved toward the house, his gaze checking everything from the footprints in the dust on the porch to the way the door hung open, not enough for a person to enter without pushing it a little further into the house. Without touching the door, he looked through the opening into the little house. Sunlight poured through a broken window, making a pattern across the wooden floor. As he studied the room through the narrow gap, a shiny glint caught his attention, so thin he nearly missed it. He focused all his attention on the spot where sunlight had glanced off something.

There it was again.

Sunshine hit a thin wire stretched across the room, not quite a foot off the ground.

Carter's pulse kicked into overdrive, and he swore. It was a goddamn tripwire.

Slowly, he backed toward the porch steps, turned and eased down the steps he'd walked up so unaware just moments before. He glanced in all directions, searching for more trip wires, finding none. He didn't trust that the one behind the door was all that had been planted. They could have set IEDs in the ground and were watching for an opportune time to detonate them.

Carter picked up the pace, arriving at the truck in the fewest steps possible. Once inside, he backed up fifty yards and shifted into park. He pulled out his cell phone and called Stone.

"Stone, we have a problem," Carter started the conversation.

"Give it to me," Stone said.

"Someone who knows what he's doing set a trip-wire just inside the front door of Amanda's cottage."

"Holy shit, Carter. Are you and your fiancée all right?"

"We are. The open front door tipped us off to trouble. We didn't go inside, but something has to be done to decommission whatever explosives they have attached to the tripwire."

As he spoke to Stone, he fired up the truck engine.

That was when he noticed the trees around the

little cottage swaying in a slight breeze. A gust of wind kicked up a dust devil and swirled it toward the structure.

His pulse leaped. "Get down!" Carter slammed the truck into reverse and hit the accelerator. He reached across, grabbed Amanda's shoulder and shoved her head down to her knees. They hadn't gone more than thirty yards when—

Boom!

"What the hell?" Amanda called out, her voice muffled against her legs.

"Tripwire in your house. The wind blew open the door and triggered it." He sat up, allowing her to do the same. Then he frowned. "Was the house all-electric, or did you have gas for heat or hot water?"

"Gas for heat and hot water," she said.

He didn't have time to hit the accelerator. The second explosion rocked the truck, and pieces of the little cottage peppered the metal body and the windshield.

"Is that all?" Amanda asked before sitting up this time.

"Should be," Carter said, sitting up to look at what was left.

The explosives had destroyed the front entrance to the cottage, leaving a gaping hole in the living room. The second explosion had leveled what was left.

"Oh, sweet Jesus." Amanda pressed her fingers to

her lips and stared wide-eyed at the mess. "You could've triggered that wire."

He'd thought about that, too. "I need to be even more careful. Had I been in that explosion, you would be on your own until Stone or Hank found another bodyguard to protect you."

"I don't want another bodyguard." She frowned fiercely. "I want you. Alive."

He reached across to take her hand. "I expect Stone will have notified the state bomb squad. We won't need them now."

Amanda nodded. "I guess we won't be getting that change of clothing."

Carter shook his head. "Even if anything is salvageable, you can't go in there. It's not safe."

She sighed. "I hate that they destroyed my cottage and all my things. Then again," she shrugged, "they're just things. The people who are suffering are more important in the long run."

"From where I'm sitting, you're one of those people suffering." He squeezed her hand.

"I'll make the call to 911." Amanda notified the 911 operator of the location of the explosion and that no one had been injured.

A few minutes later, sirens sounded from not far away as the Fort Washakie Fire Department mobilized, heading their way.

One of Joe's police officers pulled in before the

fire department arrived and questioned them about what had happened.

By the time they could leave, it was well past noon.

"I'm hungry," Carter said. "Let's grab something to eat and look for the next people on your list of Young Wolves."

"I could do with some food. There's a little café around the corner from the police station. They have a good lunch menu."

He drove to the café and parked.

They chose a table near a window and ordered burgers and fries.

While they waited for food, Carter asked, "Did any of the names on the sheet the councilwoman gave you ring a bell? Do we need to check out any of them after we interview the other teens?"

"I don't know." Amanda's brow dipped. "What do you think?"

"We got the list hoping to locate the undercover DEA agent. Stone thinks we need to stay out of his way, or we'll blow his cover."

"I'd like to know who it is, just to satisfy my curiosity." She pulled the sheet of paper out of her back pocket and studied it. "There are quite a few on the list. Checking them out could take a while."

Amanda's cell phone rang. "That's Wanda from the tribal council." She answered. "Hey, Wanda. Yes,

I'm all right. The house? It's completely destroyed. No, I'm not sure what happened… Me, too. This day could've ended much worse. Yes, I'm lucky to have Carter." Amanda shot a crooked grin toward her fake fiancé. "No, I haven't had a chance to check out the teens on the list. Two more? Sure." Amanda pulled out a pen and touched it to a blank area on the list of names. Yes, I have a pen. Go ahead." She listened carefully and wrote two names on the sheet.

"Thank you, Wanda. I will." Amanda ended the call and looked down at the names on the sheet. "She gave me two more names that weren't on the list because they didn't officially register. They just showed up. A Stacey Bending Willow and Eddie Black Bear." She looked across the table at Carter.

"Eddie," Carter said, his eyes narrowing.

Amanda nodded. "From the casino. Do you think he's the undercover DEA agent?"

"Let me have Swede do some digging on the man." Carter keyed in his request for a background check on Eddie Black Bear and sent it to Swede. Within seconds, he had a response of *K*. "Eddie seemed a little more than just a janitor by the way he spoke to Nighthawk, his supposed boss."

"We can't go back to the casino." Amanda grimaced. "I might have come on a little strong with Trevor Spotted Elk."

Carter chuckled. "I thought you were going to tear into Trevor."

"I almost did. I still think he wasn't telling me the whole truth. Maybe it was flat-out lying or lying by omission. If Eddie is the undercover DEA, why would he embed with the casino?"

"As a janitor, you can be kind of invisible. He could be working the casino during the day, listening to all the gossip from the staff there and then he can be part of gang activities at night."

Amanda nodded. "That makes sense. He's gathering information from multiple sources."

"Do you feel confident we've found our DEA agent?" Carter asked.

"About 89% confident. I'd love to question him but understand the need to keep his identity secret." She folded the sheet of paper and shoved it into her back pocket. "Well then, we start with the other Young Wolves as it would make more sense for me to want to contact them as the teen reservation counselor. Especially considering the recent rash of suicides."

"Who do you want to start with?" Carter asked.

"Nina Sweetwater," Amanda said.

The waitress chose that moment to appear with their burgers and fries. "Are you friends of Nina's?" she asked as she laid their plates on the table in front of them.

"Acquaintances," Amanda corrected. "We'd like to talk to her and make sure she's all right."

"She was here a little while ago with the same

man Tobi Running Fox had dinner with the night he committed suicide."

Carter stiffened. "Do you know who that man was?"

The waitress's brow wrinkled. "I'm sure my granddaughter would know. He's probably a gang member. He has his hair shaved on the sides but long on the top and down the back. He keeps it in a braid. It's the tattoos. Good lord, if he spent half as much on education as he did on those tattoos, he'd have a degree and a good job."

"What kind of tattoos?" Carter asked.

The waitress looked to the corner of the room, her eyes squinting as if remembering. "Grizzlies and wolves. He has what looks like a bear paw scratch tattooed across the top of one of his hands." She looked back at Carter. "I wanted to tell Nina to go home and steer clear of guys like that. They usually mean trouble."

"Did they leave together?" Amanda asked.

The waitress shook her head. "No. I watched her climb into a compact car. He rode out on a motorcycle. I remember because the motorcycle was really loud, and I was glad she didn't go with him." She looked from Amanda to Carter and back. "You think she's in trouble?"

Amanda smiled. "No. We're just curious. Do you know where Nina lives? We could go check on her. I was hired to counsel teens."

"Maybe you could counsel her on steering clear of gangs. We've lost too many recently to suicide. We can't lose more." Her gaze went to two men entering the café. "I'd better get back to work."

"Where does Nina live? We'll go check on her."

"Oh, yeah." She turned back to Amanda. "Nina lives behind the elementary school in a little house with her father. He was a good man when her mother was alive. Since she passed, he's done nothing but drink. He lost his job at the casino and now relies on Nina to work to buy groceries and pay the light bill. Such a shame." The waitress hurried away to assist other customers.

Carter hurried through his food, anxious to go by Nina's place to make sure she was all right.

Amanda was equally quick with her meal, eating only half her burger before pushing her plate aside. "Ready?" she asked, tossing her napkin on top of the other half of her burger.

Carter nodded. He tossed several bills on the table to cover the cost of their meal and a tip. They left the café and hurried to his truck. He climbed into the driver's side while Amanda helped herself into the passenger seat.

Amanda directed him toward the elementary school and onto the road that circled behind the school to a street filled with small, clapboard houses that all needed paint. What paint still clung to the boards was chipped, peeling or just not there.

A compact car stood out in front of one of the little houses.

"The waitress didn't say which house," Carter noted.

"No, but that's a compact car. I'll knock on the door and ask where we can find Nina. If she lives there…bonus. If not, someone will point us in the right direction."

Carter frowned. "I'm going with you."

She shook her head. "I can do this on my own. You'll be within a few feet. I don't want to scare her off by having two people come to speak with her."

"I don't like it. I'm supposed to protect you. I can't do that if I'm not with you."

"You will be—just a few steps away." She leaned across the cab and brushed her lips across his. "I'll be right back."

Against his better judgment, Carter stayed in the truck while Amanda walked up to the little house and knocked on the door.

A man answered, wearing jeans and no shirt or shoes. He smelled of booze, and his belly hung over the waistband of his pants. "I'm not buying anything."

Amanda smiled. "I'm not selling anything. I'm Amanda Small, the youth counselor for the reservation. I'd like to speak with Nina if she's home."

"She's busy."

"Is she here? I only want a few minutes. It won't take long. I want to make sure she's okay."

The man scowled. "You think she's not okay here with me? Fuck you. She's my daughter. You can't take her from me."

"No, sir. I'm not here to take her away. I'm worried about her since her friend died. It's a lot to process. I wanted to make sure she's handling it."

"My girl lost her mother when she was twelve. She knows what it's like to lose a loved one. She doesn't need a shrink to tell her how to feel."

"It's okay, Dad," a soft voice said behind the man. "Let me talk with her for a few minutes. The water has to come to a boil before I can cook the noodles. I'll be right outside on the porch." She touched her father's arm. "I'll be okay. Let me talk to Ms. Small."

Her father swayed a little, his eyes narrowing. "You don't need no shrink."

The teen smiled at him. "No, I don't. I have you. We muddle through just fine on our own."

"Damn right, we do." Her father glared at Amanda. "Five minutes."

Nina stepped around her father. "Could you keep an eye on the stove just in case the water bubbles over?"

Her father turned into the house, muttering something about not being a damned cook.

Nina stepped out onto the porch and closed the door behind her. "Hi, Ms. Small. What can I do for you?"

Amanda sat on the top step and patted the space

beside her. "I know we haven't spoken much, but I wanted you to know I'm here and available anytime if you need to talk about anything."

"I know." She sank onto the step beside Amanda. "Tara says good things about you. I've meant to come by your office, but I'm pretty busy with school, work and…" she cast a glance toward the door, "home."

Amanda smiled. "I know it's hard to juggle everything. I've been worried about the group of youths who call themselves the Young Wolves."

Nina's mouth formed a tight line. "Yeah. It's been bad."

"If you ever feel depressed and need someone to lean on…"

Nina's brow dipped low. "They didn't commit suicide."

Amanda nodded. "That's the message I'm getting."

"And they didn't do drugs. I don't care what they found in their bodies. They were clean. Someone had to have given them the meth without their knowledge or forced it on them." Her fists clenched in her lap. "It's all just a mess and a waste. We never should've—" Nina stopped talking and stared down at her clenched fists. "It doesn't matter now. We can't change what's happening."

"Yes, you can." Amanda leaned forward and touched the girl's arm. "Tell me what's going on. I will help."

"I can't, and you can't. No one can help us."

"Are they threatening to hurt you if you tell anyone anything?" Amanda whispered.

Nina looked up, scanning the street in front of her and nearby homes. "You should leave."

"Please, Nina. Anything little thing you can tell us might help us help you."

She shook her head. "The Young Wolves depend on me keeping my mouth shut. Their lives depend on it. My life depends on them keeping their mouths shut. Stray outside that promise and…well, you know what happens." She started to rise. "I can't help you. You can't help me. Just leave."

"Tell me one thing," Amanda persisted. "You met with someone at the café earlier. Someone with tattoos and his head shaved. You won't be telling me much since I'm sure if I asked around, others know who his. Tell me his name and save me some time."

She stared at her hands and then whispered without moving her lips. "Colt Kickingwoman." She stood and spun toward the door. "Please, don't come back. It upsets my father."

"If you need anything, come to my office, or call me." She rose from the step and handed Nina one of her cards. "I'll answer day or night. I want to help."

She shook her head. "It's too late." Then she was through the door, closing it with a firm click of the deadbolt sliding into place.

Amanda returned to the truck, climbed into the passenger seat and nodded. "Let's go."

Carter shifted into drive and pulled away from the house. He had to drive to the end of the cul-de-sac to turn around.

As they passed the Sweetwater house, a face appeared at the corner of one of the windows in front.

Nina watched them as they drove away.

"I was two seconds away from coming to get you," Carter said.

"Nina's father?" Amanda shook her head. "People handle grief differently."

"Nina's father is not handling it well," he said, frowning.

"No, but Nina loves him and doesn't want anything bad to happen to him."

"I take it she didn't have much to share?" Carter looked her way.

"The Young Wolves can't talk. If someone talks, something could happen to other members of the group. They're afraid and feel trapped."

"She said all that?" Carter asked.

"In so many words, yes." Amanda looked out the window. "She did tell me who she met at the café."

"Let me guess—Colt Kickingwoman."

Amanda frowned. "How did you know?"

"My bet is that he came to reinforce the need for her and her buddies to keep quiet about what's happening. He probably threatened her, her family or her friends."

"We need to talk to Colt," Amanda said.

"Even if we could find him, it might not be a good idea. He's sure to have people around him to protect him."

"I have you," she said.

"While you were talking with Nina, I spoke with Swede. He did a background check on Eddie Black Bear."

Amanda cocked an eyebrow. "And?"

"He's working in Anchorage, Alaska. Apparently, he checked in this morning and every workday without missing one for the past two years."

"Our Eddie is either the undercover DEA agent or an inside contact for whoever is supplying the drugs to the reservation. Assuming this is all about drug trafficking." She shook her head. "These people have enough strikes against them; they don't need a massive drug cartel calling the shots and funneling more drugs onto the rez."

"Let's hope Hank comes through with a plan to clean this mess up."

"I don't see how anyone can. It could be completely overwhelming for any organization."

"The people who work with Hank have been known to face some of the worst odds against over-whelming enemy forces that were hard to find and entrenched in their country and communities. We did all right."

She reached for his hand and held onto it. "Tomorrow will be the test. Either we all pass, or we all fail. I hope the teens make it out alive."

CHAPTER 13

WITH THE SUN setting on the reservation, Carter drove back into Fort Washakie. "We should get a room for the night."

"You're right. What can two people do to stop what's about to take place when we don't even know what it is?" Amanda said. "I feel so powerless."

"I'll get on the phone with my people and see what they have planned. Hopefully, they'll come through for us."

"For Nina, Tara, Keme and their families." She lifted her chin. "For the good of the Arapaho and Shoshoni people. I refuse to feel hopeless about the fate of my people. As a race, we've faced overwhelming odds and survived. We are resilient. Though we could use a little help right now." She smiled as Carter pulled into a hotel parking lot filled with cars from other states. Families of tourists eager to experience the Native American culture.

"Will this be all right with you?" Carter left the truck engine running.

She shrugged. "It's as good a hotel as any. I wonder if we're too close to the factions tearing my people apart. And I mean, physically. I have no idea where the NA Syndicate or the Lords of Arapaho base their operations. Are they near Fort Washakie or the larger town of Riverton? Or somewhere else entirely? With over 2.2 million acres to choose from, they could be anywhere."

"I would think they'd be close enough to the major towns to attract members who want to join."

"So, they could be close to here." She shivered. "Since I'm obviously a target, I'll sleep with one eye open. Hopefully, they won't attempt to blow up the hotel." She frowned. "Maybe we should go sleep at the police station. I'd hate for innocent people to be hurt because I chose to be selfish and stay at a hotel when I'm the target of terrorists." She shook her head. "No. We can't stay here—not after they blew up my house. We'll have to stay at the police department. We should be safe there." She glanced in Carter's direction. "Are you okay with that? Or better yet, you can stay here at the hotel, and I'll stay at the police department."

He touched a finger to her lips. "I'm with you all the way."

She kissed the finger and raised her hand to cup his against her cheek. "Thank you for having my back, or front for that matter. If I'd been first through the front door of my house, I wouldn't be sitting here in your truck wishing you were kissing me again."

He brushed his thumb across her lips. "There's probably not going to be much privacy in the station."

"We could risk it and stay here," she suggested, all the while shaking her head. "No. I would feel horrible if someone got hurt because of me. Though making love with you is top of my list of desires, maybe if we abstain tonight. We'll have more incentive to stay alive tomorrow night at Alkali Lake."

"Incentive be damned. I don't need it. I need you. Now." Carter leaned close and captured her mouth with his in a deep, soul-defining kiss that left him breathless and wanting so much more.

Carter stared at the hotel in front of him, his core heating with the natural and insistent desire he felt for Amanda. "We could stay here for the first half of the night and move to the police station for the remainder."

Amanda grinned. "I like the way you think. Come on. Let's get checked in for the first half of our night."

Carter rounded the truck and opened her door for her.

Amanda dropped eagerly down into his arms and laced her fingers behind his neck. She kissed him soundly and then broke away. "I'm saving the best for behind closed doors."

"I'm counting on it."

They got the last available room located on the third floor.

Amanda's first move was to claim the bathroom.

Carter paced the room and peeked out the window several times, wondering if they were making a big mistake or if he was worrying too much.

When Amanda finally emerged from the bath-room, she wore nothing but a bath towel and a grin. "I showered then hand-washed my clothes. Sorry, they're hanging everywhere to dry."

"It'll be fine; I might do the same. Promise me you won't unlock that door for anyone." Armed with the toothbrush and toothpaste they'd acquired at the hotel in Riverton, he took his turn in the bathroom, showered, shaved and brushed his teeth. He didn't like leaving her in the other room for any length of time. Still dripping from his shower, he wrapped the towel around his hips and stepped out to check on Amanda.

She lay in the bed, the sheets and comforter pulled up to her chin, her eyes closed.

Carter's heart swelled. Though his cock was hard and ready, he didn't have the heart to wake her. She'd been through so much.

He dropped his towel, climbed between the sheets

and pulled her gently against him, careful not to wake her. If they weren't going to make love yet, the least he could be satisfied with was holding her in his arms. Naked body against naked body.

His cock pressed into her hip. Carter swallowed a groan and tried to relax and sleep, even if for only half the night. Maybe they could sleep there the entire night and not bring their misfortune to the hotel's other guests.

Her hands settled on his chest and smoothed a path down to his abdomen.

Carter grinned. "Not asleep after all?"

"I was but opted for a little awake time with you." Her fingers wrapped around his cock, and the fun began.

They spent the next two hours exploring each other's bodies and making love like there would be no tomorrow.

For that matter, if the event the teens alluded to was really that big and heavily armed, there might not be a tomorrow for a lot of them.

All the more reason to enjoy the present and spend as much time with each other as they could. If they died tomorrow, Carter would only regret not having more time with Amanda. He wouldn't regret meeting her or turning his world upside down to spend their last minutes together.

Knowing they needed to move to a safer location halfway through the night didn't stop them from falling asleep in each other's arms. It wasn't until the incessant screeching of a fire alarm blasted through the hotel's speaker system that Carter realized just how asleep they'd been.

"What the hell?" Amanda grumbled when Carter shook her away.

"Get dressed quickly," he said. "The fire alarm's going off."

"Do you smell smoke?" she said, her eyes still closed.

"No."

"Then it's not a real fire. Sleep." She rolled over in the sheets and sighed.

He ran to the bathroom, where she'd hung her clothes to dry. Some items were still damp, but for the most part, they were close enough to dry to wear. Given they were the only clothes they had, they'd have to do.

Carter hurried back to the bed and pressed a kiss to Amanda's bare shoulder. "Seriously, we can't risk it. If it's a fire, we're on the third floor. We need to get down the stairwells before it spreads."

Amanda moaned and sat up, the sheet falling around her waist.

Carter dragged her shirt over her head in an attempt to get her dressed and out of the room.

"Bra," she said.

He handed her the bra and waited while she

quickly hooked it in place and shoved her hands through the blouse.

He took her hand and helped her out of bed and onto her feet.

She finished dressing and pulled on her shoes. "Let's go," she said, sounding awake and ready to get the hell out of the building before it burned to the ground.

Carter took her hand and led her out of the room and down the hallway to the stairwell.

"I don't smell any smoke," Amanda said. "It's probably a false alarm."

"False or not, I'd rather err on the cautious side," Carter said, pushing open the stairwell door.

They arrived at the ground floor behind the other guests, dressed in a varying array of pajamas, bathrobes and wrinkled clothing.

The night manager directed people away from the building. "Please move to the other side of the parking lot until the fire department gives us the all-clear.

Sleepy people moaned and groused about being awakened from their sleep by malfunctioning fire alarms.

Amanda and Carter had just stepped out the side door of the hotel when a young woman ran up behind them and plowed into Carter. "Please," she said. "Help me."

Carter spun to find Tara Running Fox clinging to his sleeve.

"Tara, what's wrong?" Amanda asked.

"Oh, Amanda," she cried and threw herself into Amanda's arms. "It's Keme. He's injured and in a room on the second floor. I couldn't get him out of bed. He's too heavy and can't help himself down the stairs. Please, help us."

Carter frowned. "What room?"

Tara gave him the room number and her card key. "Hurry. I swear I smelled smoke. There really is a fire."

Carter started for the building. When Amanda and Tara followed, he stopped and faced them. "You two stay out here and join the others on the far side of the parking lot. I'll get Keme and bring him down."

"You'll need help," Tara insisted.

Carter shook his head. "You'll help more by staying here where it's safe." He met Amanda's gaze with a stern glance.

She nodded. "I'll make sure Tara gets to the other side of the parking lot. Hurry and be careful."

He bent and pressed a kiss to her lips. "I'll be right back."

He didn't like leaving them out there in the dark with the chaos of an evacuating a hotel. Sirens sounded in the distance as Carter ran back inside the building and up the staircase he'd just come down. He got off at the second floor, found the right room and used the key card to unlock the door.

Inside, a young man with dark hair and darker eyes lay on the bed, bruised, bloody and with his jeans torn away from the knee down on his left leg.

"Keme?"

He looked at Carter through swollen eyes. "Yeah."

"I'm here to get you out of here."

He shook his head. "Can't move. I think my leg is broken."

"Why the hell didn't you go straight to the hospital?" Carter said.

"Couldn't. That would expose Tara. They can't take her. They'll use her to get to me and the rest of the group."

"Well, it looks like they got to you."

"Yeah," Keme said.

"We're getting you out of this building. There's a fire alarm going off. Everyone has to leave the premises." He approached the bed and took one of Keme's hands in preparation for slinging the man over his back like a sack of potatoes.

Keme held back. "Where's Tara?"

"In the parking lot with Amanda and the other guests from the hotel."

"They'll take her. Leave me here. Go make sure she's okay."

"I will after I get you out of the building."

"No, you have to protect Tara. She's in danger."

Carter had to admit he wasn't pleased with leaving the two women in the parking lot without anyone to protect them. He just had to get back down there before anything happened. "Sorry, man, but this will like hurt like hell." He bent, pulled Keme over his shoulder and lifted.

Keme cried out when his leg jarred and his ribs hit Carter's shoulder. Then he was silent, probably passed out and a complete dead weight. Carter headed for the stairwell, the young man's weight slowing his progress.

By the time he reached the ground floor, he was breathing hard, sweating and his knees hurt.

Across the parking lot, he spied Amanda and Tara near a couple of vehicles. He started to cross to them, but the fire engine chose that moment to pull into the parking lot and park between the hotel and where the guests had evacuated.

An ambulance arrived right behind the fire engine. Carter carried Keme to the ambulance. As soon as they unloaded a gurney, Carter eased his burden onto clean white sheets and straightened the kinks out of his back.

When he turned toward Amanda and Tara, they'd disappeared.

AMANDA HAD DONE as she'd promised, taking Tara across the parking lot. She'd rather have gone with

Carter. After spending all her time in his company, she wanted to spend more and missed him when she couldn't.

The blare of a siren filled the air. The fire engine pulled into the parking lot and blocked Amanda's view of the hotel's side door where Carter had reentered. Though the fire truck's siren ceased upon arrival, another siren wailed on its way toward the hotel.

A white van backed out of a parking space and rolled slowly through the lot, passing between Amanda and the fire truck.

Suddenly, it stopped, the side door slid open and two men leaped out.

Amanda shoved Tara behind her, but it was too late.

The first man grabbed Amanda and dragged her into the van.

Though she screamed, the arriving ambulance drowned out her cries. Amanda landed on her hands and knees. Before she could attempt to scramble back out of the van, Tara flew through the door, landing on top of Amanda.

The two men jumped in, the door slammed shut and the van pulled out of the parking lot.

Tara rolled off Amanda and threw herself at one of the men. "Let me out!" she yelled.

The man backhanded her, knocking her against the side wall.

Amanda rose into a crouching position. While the attention was on Tara, she launched herself into the other man's gut, slamming him into the side of the van. He cursed and swung a fist, catching Amanda in the jaw. The blow sent her flying across the van. Her head hit the wall. Pain sliced through her head. Though she fought against it, a fog of darkness engulfed her, and she sank to the floor.

She couldn't have been out long. But it was long enough. The van was still moving. She wasn't. Her wrists had been bound with duct tape and a strip had been applied across her mouth.

Tara lay beside her, similarly bound and out cold.

Amanda didn't know where they were taking her or what they planned to do with the two women. All she could do was pray people had seen what had happened and would let Carter know.

CARTER SCANNED the sea of tired faces, looking for the beauty who was quickly stealing his heart. He didn't see her, but she might have moved back to blend into the crowd, impatiently awaiting the all-clear signal so they could all return to their rooms and what was left of the night for sleep.

His heart racing, Carter ran to the edge of the crowd and scanned every face, searching for Amanda. The more he looked, the more he realized it wasn't likely he'd find them there.

He asked a woman standing near the last point where he'd seen Amanda and Tara. "There were two women standing near you a moment ago. Both with dark hair. Did you see where they went?"

The woman frowned. "There was so much going on. I think there was a white van. It passed me when the ambulance came in. Men got out, and I think they helped the ladies inside. I was watching the ambulance. I'm not sure."

"Did you happen to see a license plate?"

She shook her head. "No."

Carter asked others who were standing around. Some had seen a white van, but most had been watching smoke coming out of the far side of the hotel or the firefighters unrolling the hose from their truck.

While their attention had been on the smoke and first responders, Tara and Amanda had been taken.

CHAPTER 14

CARTER'S CELL phone vibrated in his back pocket. He pulled it out, checked the name on the screen and answered, "Carter, here."

"Know it's late, but I wanted to let you know the team is on its way. We'll be there by morning."

"Good." He rubbed his eyes. "Amanda's gone. I'll need your help getting her back."

Stone cursed. "What happened?"

Carter filled him in while pacing the parking lot. His truck was blocked in by the fire engine, and the firefighters were just getting started putting out the fire.

"Sounds like they set up a diversion to get their hands on the women."

"That was the conclusion I came to. They'll probably use them as hostages to buy them safe passage out."

"Good news is that Hank's made contact with the DEA, Homeland Security and Bureau of Indian Affairs," Stone said. "Still not sure what they're sending yet, but Hank's pulling in everyone he can. His team will be at the target location tonight."

Carter's cell phone beeped in his ear, indicating another incoming call—this one from Swede. "Stone, I have a call coming in from Hank's computer guy. Let me know when you get close. We'll arrange a meeting location away from town."

"Will do. Out here," Stone said.

Carter answered Swede's incoming call. "Carter, here."

"I know it's late, but I thought you'd like to know what I found."

"I do. Anything you can give me will be more than I have. They set up a diversion, and while I was helping someone else, they got Amanda and Tara, the teen whose family we helped to relocate."

"Damn," Swede said. "Sorry to hear that. Hopefully, some of the pieces will start falling in place, and we can get them back."

"What did you find?" Carter asked.

"I poked around some more and dug deeper into the DEA data and found our agent. I know you said he's posing as Eddie Black Bear, who actually lives up in Alaska, but his real name is Ernest Perez. He's been with the DEA for seven years, working as a field agent for the past five. He was involved in a job down in Guatemala that went sideways. Two other DEA agents were killed, Perez was injured, and the money and drugs disappeared. They eventually found where the drugs went by questioning the locals who hauled it, but the money was never recovered. It was all kind of sketchy, but they didn't have any other witnesses to corroborate Perez's story. They had to take him at his word."

"What kind of injury did he sustain?" Carter asked.

"He had a knot on his head. He claimed they hit him hard enough he was knocked out. When he came to, the other two agents had been shot and the drugs and money were gone."

"Convenient," he muttered.

"Since then, his record has been clean. When the Bureau of Indian Affairs asked for help with the drug trafficking on the Wind River Reservation, Perez volunteered. Since he had the right coloring and facial structure, he could pass for Native American. He went undercover eight months ago and only checks in once a month."

"Think he's gone bad?"

"I wouldn't swear to it, but it all smells fishy. Since you mentioned he was with the casino manager and Trevor Spotted Elk, I ran checks on both of them and on Colt Kickingwoman." Swede paused. "Colt Kickingwoman has a bank account in Riverton. He received a number of transfers from an account in the Caymans. That account is under C. Jones. Something similar happened with Trevor. He's been receiving transfers from an account in the Caymans under the name T. Smith."

"Were you able to follow the money in those Cayman accounts back to its origin?"

"It took some digging," Swede said. "Eventually, I traced it to TN Enterprises. All the accounts were set up fairly recently. Smith and Jones, within the past three months. TN Enterprises, seven months ago."

Carter's hand tightened on the cell phone. "Shortly after Perez's arrival. Let me guess, TN stands for Theo Nighthawk?"

"I checked his local accounts," Swede said. "I didn't find any connection to TN Enterprises. There were some wire transfers from an investment company based in Switzerland. I couldn't trace them back from there. I also discovered that he used his credit card to make plane reservations to Cuba. From Vancouver."

"Why would Nighthawk fly from Vancouver? Unless he plans on making a run for the border. When is the flight?"

"The day after tomorrow," Swede said.

Carter watched as firefighters extinguished whatever it was that had caused the smoke. "What about Perez?"

"All I found on him was the account where his

paycheck is deposited. He hasn't touched it in months."

"Sounds like Colt, Trevor and Theo are in cahoots."

"The jury is still out on Perez. He may or may not be involved."

"What's your gut telling you?" Carter asked.

"I wouldn't trust him," Swede said. "I gave all this information to Hank. He's asked his contact at the DEA to keep their plans from Perez or anyone who might contact him."

"Good."

"When you get the chance, check the hotel security cameras. You might catch the white van in the video. I can run a trace on the license plate."

"As long as the security room isn't what was on fire, I will."

"I'll be here whenever you have something," Swede said.

"Do you ever sleep?"

Swede laughed. "I do, with one hand on my keyboard. Be safe, brother."

"Will do. And thanks." Carter ended the call about the time the firefighters started rolling up the hose.

He checked with the man in charge.

"The fire was contained in a large waste bin at the rear of the hotel," the chief reported. "No smoke or fire damage has been reported inside. The crew has performed a thorough sweep of the rooms and hasn't found any damage. These people can return to their rooms whenever they like."

Carter nodded. It had definitely been a diversion. And it had done the job.

Tara had been taken to secure the loyalty and silence of the Young Wolves. Amanda had been taken as leverage to keep Carter and the people behind him from interfering with the transfer that night.

The people who'd taken them didn't know who they'd just pissed off.

As soon as the firefighters gave the all-clear, Carter made sure he was the first person into the hotel. He headed straight for the front desk, where a harried night manager braced himself to handle the disgruntled customers streaming in from the parking lot.

"I need to see the footage on your video monitoring system," he said.

The night manager frowned. "I'm sorry. I'm not allowed to grant access to the data."

Carter planted his hands on the desk and leaned closer. "My fiancé was kidnapped during this fiasco. Every minute that passes, she's being taken further away. I don't have time to get a search warrant."

"I'm sorry—"

"Sorry isn't going to get her back. If this was your girlfriend, wife, daughter or sister, would you stand back and wait for her to disappear forever?"

The night manager shook his head.

"I need to see the vehicle that got away with her. There has to be an image with the license plate on it."

"I can't let you look." The manager held up his hand. "I can search through the footage for you." He snagged one of the clerks. "You'll have to manage the desk. I have to help this customer." He motioned for Carter to follow him into the room behind the counter and sat at a desk with a large monitor with an array of eight video images displayed.

Over the next fifteen minutes, the night manager searched the footage of the parking lot and the exterior of the building, looking for the white van.

Carter moved to stand behind him, growing more anxious with every passing minute. When he saw the ghostly image of a white van pausing beside the trash bin, he said, "There!"

The night manager backed up and replayed the video. The van opened on the opposite side, but Carter could see the shadowy images of a man dressed in black running toward the waste bin with a lighted Molotov cocktail in his hand. He opened the lid, tossed the bottle into the bin and ran back to the van. With that time in mind, they searched through the footage of the other sides of the building and found the white van backed into a parking space at the rear of the complex.

When the footage played forward, the van eventually left the space and moved slowly out of range of the camera. Switching to the next camera, they were able to follow it to where the fire truck blocked the camera.

Moments later, the van emerged from behind the truck and drove toward the exit.

When it turned to leave the parking lot, the license plate came into view.

The manager froze the screen and zoomed in. The image was fuzzy, but the numbers and letters could be discerned. Carter jotted them on a piece of paper. "Thank you," he said and hurried out of the hotel.

Once outside, he called Swede and gave him the license plate number.

"I'm on it," Swede said. "I'll get right back to you."

The fire truck was just pulling out of the parking lot.

Carter wanted to jump into his truck and search for the white van, but he knew it would do very little good. Driving around a 2.2-million-acre reservation would be a waste of time. However, staying put would make him crazy.

As the sun rose on the day of reckoning, Carter climbed into his truck and drove to the Wind River Police station to report Amanda and Tara's kidnapping. Not that they would have any more luck finding them, already understaffed and now down one experienced leader.

Knowing it might be a futile effort, Carter drove around Fort Washakie, hoping to catch a glimpse of a white van. After his first pass, he received a text from Swede. The van was registered to the casino in Riverton.

Carter turned around and drove to Riverton and the casino there. When he arrived, he circled the casino several times before parking and going inside.

Open twenty-four-seven, the lights were just as bright in the morning as they were at night, and there were customers at the slot machines.

He didn't see Theo Nighthawk or Eddie Black Bear. The only security guard moving through the rooms was a rotund man with a short haircut and no tattoos.

Carter ducked through a door marked "Authorized Personnel Only" and walked down a hall with doors on both sides. Most were locked. One had Theo Nighthawk's name on it.

The door was locked, and there wasn't a light on inside.

Carter pulled a pocket knife out of his pocket and tried sliding it into the doorjamb. It wouldn't fit. The door had an RFID scanner and wouldn't open without the correct card.

If Theo Nighthawk was involved in the drug trafficking, he wouldn't keep any records in his office at the casino. Carter didn't know what he expected to find.

"Sir, this is a restricted area," a female voice called out behind him.

He turned to find a waitress standing at the end of the hallway.

"Sorry. I was looking for the men's room."

"I'll show you where it is," she said and waited for him to follow her back into the game room.

She led him to another hallway where the restrooms were located and left him to return to her duty station.

Carter went into the restroom, washed his hands and stared at his face in the mirror. How had he let this happen? Amanda had been his responsibility, and he'd let her down.

He left the casino and circled the outside, hoping to see the white van. When he didn't, he climbed into his truck and headed for the hospital to check on Joe Sharp Spear.

The room where Joe had been was empty.

Carter's chest tightened. He spun to find a nurse standing behind him.

"If you're looking for Joe, he's been moved out of ICU into a regular room." She smiled. "He woke up last night and hollered for a hamburger. The doctor checked him out this morning and said he would be fine once his injuries healed." She gave him the room number.

Carter took the elevator down and found the room.

Joe was inside, arguing with the nurse. "Damn it, I'm fine. I want my pants. I have work to do."

When Carter entered, Joe shifted his attention. "Oh, good. Someone who might actually help. Carter, I need my pants. Can you get these wardens to find them for me?"

"What's the issue?"

"I can't leave the hospital in a gown, flashing my ass at everyone."

"Has the doctor cleared you to leave?" Carter asked.

"Hell, no. He wants to keep me another night. I told him I was fine. I have work to do." Joe's frown deepened. "Where's Amanda?"

Carter sucked in a breath and let it out slowly before answering. "She's missing, along with Tara Running Fox."

Joe quit blustering and stared at Carter through his one uninjured eye. "They got her, didn't they?" He muttered a curse.

"Someone did. Any idea who might have taken her?" Carter stared at the man who'd been more of a father to Amanda than her own.

"Yes. What day is it?" Joe demanded.

"Saturday."

Joe cursed again. "Find me my damned pants, or I'm walking out of here in my birthday suit."

The nurse tipped her head toward the closet in the corner.

Carter looked inside and found a plastic bag filled with Joe's clothes and shoes. He handed them to the man, wondering if he was doing the right thing.

Joe glared at the nurse. "Get out."

She scurried out the door and let it swing closed behind her.

Joe sat up and swung his legs over the side of the bed.

He swayed, his eyes rolled back, and he started to slide off the bed.

Carter dove for him, catching the man beneath his arms before he hit the floor. He helped him back into the hospital bed and pulled the sheet up around him. "Joe, you need to give it another night before you try to leave."

"I don't have another night. This is the night I need to be at work."

"Why tonight?" Carter asked, wanting to know how much Joe was aware of.

"There's a massive drug deal going down tonight. I was on my way back to the station after I got the word from Trevor Spotted Elk."

Carter's eyes narrowed. "Trevor told you about it? We figured he was in on it."

"He was, but he's being edged out by Theo Nighthawk and Eddie Black Bear. They're keeping him in the loop, but he thinks they'll kill him as soon as the deal goes down. Eddie has Colt Kickingwoman doing the dirty work for him."

"Is that who did this to you?" Carter asked.

Joe nodded. "He's just a pawn. Eddie gave him the order to kill me." Joe's lip curled. "They didn't quite succeed. They wanted me out of the way of their drug drop. Trevor told me everything he knew, hoping I could get him a plea bargain for having helped. He didn't know Eddie's plan to get me out of the way. Now that I've been in the hospital, nothing's been done to catch them or stop this from happening."

Joe tried again to sit up, only to fall back against the pillows. "And now, they have my Amanda girl." He pinched the bridge of his nose and winced. "You have to go there. They'll use her and Tara as hostages if things go sideways." He stared at Carter. "You can't let anything happen to her. She's all the family I have."

Carter squared his shoulders. "First of all, Eddie isn't really Eddie Black Bear. Eddie Black Bear lives in Anchorage, Alaska."

"I thought he looked different from when I last saw him as a kid." Joe's brow furrowed. "If he isn't Eddie, who is he?"

"Undercover DEA agent Ernest Perez. We think he's gone bad. We have plans in the works with people who make things happen. What all did Trevor tell you? I can get word to those involved in stopping this deal and catching those responsible."

Joe nodded. "I knew Amanda had a good one

when she brought you home to me. She's a smart girl. You're lucky to have her."

Carter didn't have the heart to tell Joe the engagement was a lie. "What do you know?"

"A Mexican cartel is delivering heroin-laced with fentanyl with a street value of over a million dollars. Trevor also suspects the cartel is planning to launder money through the casino. The shipment will be heavily guarded, and the drop will be completed in less than twenty minutes. The Lords are bringing trucks and trailers to the location at Alkali Lake."

Carter nodded. "That's basically what we got from Tara. That the location was Alkali Lake, and something big was going down. The Young Wolves group she belongs to is being threatened. They killed three of them to get the others to stay silent and participate in the transfer."

"I figured it was something like that. Those kids got in way over their heads."

Carter's cell phone vibrated in his pocket. He dug it out, hoping it would be Amanda or Tara, or at least the people who were holding them hostage. Then he might be able to bargain with them.

It was Stone Jacobs. "We're thirty minutes out of Fort Washakie."

"Hold on." As he stood in Joe's room at the Riverton Hospital, Carter looked over the map on his phone. "Still there?"

"Still here," Stone confirmed.

"You're going to pass through Fort Washakie and get off at the exit for Ray Lake. I'll meet you there."

"Roger. Hear anything about Amanda and Tara?"

Carter's chest tightened. "Nothing."

"We'll come up with a plan. We'll get her back," Stone promised and ended the call.

Carter turned to Joe. "I have to go." He headed for the door.

"Keep me informed," Joe called out. "Tell Amanda I love her."

"Will do." Carter left the hospital and headed for Ray Lake, south of Fort Washakie. He'd get Amanda back if he had to take down the entire Mexican cartel and the bastards helping traffic the drugs all by himself.

CHAPTER 15

THE VAN DROVE around for what felt like an eternity, though it was likely only an hour. When the driver stopped, everyone got out except Tara and Amanda. They slid the side door shut on the van, and then what sounded like an overhead garage door rattled and rolled until it extinguished what little light came through the van's front windshield.

Tara moaned and rolled onto her back. In the darkness, Amanda could see the whites of the girl's eyes when she opened them for the first time since the man had knocked her out.

With her mouth taped shut, Amanda couldn't reassure her that everything was all right. Hell, nothing was all right. They were hostages of people who didn't have a problem killing teenagers.

Amanda couldn't let them be the next victims. She pushed to a sitting position and reached her bound hands up to the tape across her mouth. After several attempts, she managed to lift one corner. She pulled the tape off, feeling like she took half her skin with it.

"Tara, hang on." Amanda leaned over the girl and worked the tape off her mouth. "Are you okay?"

Tara nodded. "I have a splitting headache, but other than that, I'm okay. Where are we?"

"I don't know. They drove for a long time. I think we're in some kind of garage or warehouse." She worked her wrists in an attempt to free them.

Tara sat up and groaned. "Bastard hit me hard."

"We have to get out of here. I don't know what they have planned for us, but it can't be good for us or anyone else we care about," Amanda said.

"I saw a video online where a woman demonstrated how to get out of tape just like this," Tara said. "She brought her arms down fast while pulling them apart at the same time."

Though Amanda couldn't see what Tara was doing, she heard her grunt as she attempted the procedure.

"I'm not exactly sure how it works. Now, I wish I'd paid more attention to the video," Tara said and grunted again. "You try it. Maybe you'll have more luck."

Amanda lifted her arms high over her head and brought them down sharply while pulling them apart.

The tape broke, and her wrists were free.

"I did it," she said.

"Great, then help me out of mine."

Amanda felt around Tara's wrists for the end of the tape and unwound it until Tara's were also free.

"What now?" Tara asked.

"We get the hell out of here," Amanda said, moving toward the front of the van to peer out of the windshield.

Wherever they were, it was dark. She couldn't see anyone moving about.

Behind her, the sliding door opened.

Amanda spun and felt her way to the opening.

Tara was already out and standing beside the van. "There's a small door on the other side of the garage door."

Faint light filtered through the cracks in the garage door, offering them enough light to make their way across the concrete floor.

When they reached the door, Amanda touched Tara's arm. "Can you hear anything outside?"

Tara pressed her ear to the metal and listened. "Nothing." She grabbed the knob and twisted it slowly, then pushed it open a crack.

Outside the building, the sun shone brightly, blinding Amanda after the darkness of the interior.

Before her vision could adjust, the door was flung open and a man stood there, glaring at them. "You'll have to do a better job securing our guests."

Amanda crouched low and rammed her shoulder

into the man's gut, knocking him backward. He fell to the ground, cursing.

Tara darted past him.

Amanda followed.

They didn't get far before half a dozen men surrounded them. One of them was covered in grizzly and wolf tattoos, with his hair shaved on the sides, long on top and down the back. He gave a wicked smile and advanced on Tara. "I'll tie them up."

"You can't play with them until after the drop," the man on the ground said. As he stood and brushed the dust off his suit, Amanda recognized him.

"You're Theo Nighthawk, the manager at the casino," Amanda said.

He dipped his head in acknowledgment. "Yes, I am."

"Why have you kidnapped us? Let us go," Amanda demanded.

The man shook his head. "Not until I no longer need you. You two are my ticket out, my free pass, my get-out-of-jail-free card."

"You were behind all this?" Tara glared at the casino manager. "You were responsible for the deaths of my friends and brother?"

Nighthawk shook his head. "I can't say that was all me. It was my partner's idea to keep the young people in line by eliminating the most vocal."

Eddie Black Bear appeared beside Nighthawk, his lip pulled back in a sneer. "They brought it on themselves," he said. "The Young Wolves, just like the Lords of Arapaho and the NA Syndicate, signed on for this operation. They all agreed to silence in exchange for the payoff. Those who reneged on the promise…paid."

Tara launched herself at Eddie. "Bastard. You killed my brother!"

Amanda went after her, but the men closest to her grabbed her before she could reach the teen.

Tara raked her fingernails down Eddie's cheeks.

Two men grabbed her from behind, pulled her away from the man and held her while she twisted and turned, kicking, yelling and trying to get to the man who'd killed Tobi. "You bastard!" she cried, tears streaming down her angry face.

Eddie touched his hand to his face. Claw marks on both sides of his cheeks bled a bright red. He stalked up to Tara and grabbed her by the throat, squeezing so hard her face turned red and then blue.

"Let go of her!" Amanda struggled against the hands holding her, but they were stronger and didn't loosen their grips. "You'll kill her!"

Eddie snorted. "That's the idea."

"We need them," Theo reminded him. "Both of them."

"One will do," Eddie said, his hold on Tara's throat relentless.

"Not if we split up," Theo said.

Eddie's eyes narrowed, and finally, he let go of Tara's neck.

The teen sagged in the clutches of the men on either side of her.

Amanda let go of the breath she'd been holding as color returned to Tara's cheeks, and she looked up.

"You'll pay," she said, her voice nothing more than a ragged croak.

"No," he said. "You will. Try that again, and I won't show you mercy. You'll be the next to fly over the edge of a cliff."

Tara glared at the man, hatred burning in her eyes.

"Colt." Eddie turned to the man with the many tattoos. "Gag them and secure them with zip-ties. If they get loose again, I'll replace you with someone who can do a better job."

Colt looked to the men holding Tara and Amanda and jerked his head toward the warehouse.

They dragged Amanda and Tara back into the warehouse, secured their wrists behind their backs with zip-ties and added zip-ties around their ankles. Then they stuffed rags in their mouths, lifted them and shoved them into the van, closing the door.

Amanda tried to spit the rag out, failing miserably.

She couldn't give up. Tara needed her to get her out of this mess. Scooting across the van floor, she searched for anything she could use to cut the zip-ties. When she failed to find a sharp edge, she figured the least she could do was get the gag out of Tara's mouth until they came up with a plan to escape.

Inching her way back to Tara, she positioned her hands close to Tara's face and fumbled with her fingers for the gag, finally pulling it free.

"That bastard," Tara said on a sob. "Here, let me get yours." She worked her way around to pull Amanda's gag from her mouth.

Lying on her side, Amanda said, "We will get out of this, Tara. And those men will get what they deserve."

"Damn right they will," Tara said, sniffling. "Do you have a plan to make that happen?"

"No, but we aren't alone in serving justice." Amanda prayed that Carter and his friends were successful in stopping these criminals from succeeding in their efforts. They needed to pay for what they'd done.

Amanda hoped she and Tara would be around to see that happen.

CARTER FELT a rush of relief when he met his team near Ray Lake. He hugged Stone and the others and told them what had happened at the hotel and what he'd learned from Joe.

"At least we know for certain this is all about drug

trafficking, and they're going to make a major drop tonight," Stone said.

Carter nodded. "We're up against two gangs, and I don't know how many will show up with the Mexican cartel."

"Well, we came bearing gifts." Stone opened the back of the SUV they'd driven over in to display an array of weapons on par with what they'd used during their time as Navy SEALs. Semi-automatic rifles with state-of-the-art scopes, submachine guns and C-4 explosives.

Carter laughed. "How did you get some of this stuff?"

"Hank has connections," Stone said. "Take what you need. And gear up with armored plating and communications. We'll be tuned into the same frequency as Hank and his crew when they arrive."

The men chose their weapons, checked their functionality and tested their radio communications. They pulled up maps and studied the terrain, identifying the best route in and out of the drop site. Not sure exactly how and when Hank and his team would arrive, they made a plan.

"I almost forgot," Bubba said. "Cookie sent food, so we didn't have to make an appearance in town." He pulled an ice chest out of the back of the SUV and opened the top. "Sandwiches, fruit, cheese and crackers…everything you could want."

Except for Amanda.

Carter couldn't eat, knowing Amanda was being held hostage. Every horrible scenario filled his head. Were they torturing her and Tara? Would the animals rape the women?

His stomach roiled. Once again, he'd failed someone he loved. This time, though, he had the opportunity to do everything in his power to get her back.

By the time the sun set, he was psyched and ready to kick ass. You didn't fuck with the people he cared about and not pay the price.

The men drove to the location they'd determined would be a good place to leave their vehicles. From there, they'd proceed on foot and establish a perimeter around the proposed drop point.

The event wasn't scheduled to take place until midnight. They would be in place well before that time, hopefully, before the gangs and the cartel moved in.

Eager to get there, Carter took point and moved quickly through scrub brush and semi-arid terrain. They didn't need the night vision goggles on their helmets. Stars shone brightly, lighting their way.

They formed a perimeter around the area where the transfer would take place. Bubba and Moe took sentry duty on the road leading in. Carter positioned himself close to the site, lying low on the ground, with not much more than a scrubby bush for concealment.

Once in place, they waited.

And waited.

Carter checked his watch every few minutes, wishing the time would pass quicker, bringing them closer to the midnight drop time.

Fifteen minutes past 11:00 pm, Bubba announced, "We have headlights on the road coming in."

"Remember, we want all of the players here before we make any moves," Carter reminded them.

"Where the hell is Hank and his team out of Eagle Rock?" Daxton Young asked.

"He said he'd be here," Stone said. "Hank keeps his promises. We wouldn't be in the States if he didn't."

"True," Carter said.

"First vehicle passed," Moe reported.

"We have visual on vehicle one," Stone reported.

Carter studied the old car chugging into the open area. Once it had stopped, three people got out and leaned against the hood. From where Carter stood, these three people appeared to be teenagers. One wore a hoodie with an image of a gray wolf emblazoned across the back, appropriate for someone belonging to an organization called Young Wolves.

At 11:25, more vehicles rolled in. Some were rental trucks. Others were trucks towing enclosed trailers. They came to the end of the little road, then backed into makeshift parking places, ready to take off at a moment's notice. A pack of motorcycle riders pulled in and set up their own perimeter, sporting rifles and handguns.

The closer it got to midnight, the more anxious Carter became. What if they didn't bring Amanda and Tara to the transfer? What if they were holding them somewhere else and threatened to kill them if the operation didn't go as planned?

So far, Hank and his men hadn't put in an appearance. When were they supposed to arrive? With just six men, Carter's team was significantly outnumbered.

Carter counted two dozen men in the field in front of him. He would bet they didn't have the combat skills Stone's team had. However, what they lacked in combat skills, they might make up for in youth and fierceness.

"Eagle Rock BroPro incoming," a deep voice said into Carter's radio headset.

"Hank. We thought you weren't going to join us for this party," Stone whispered.

"Wouldn't miss it for all the money in the world," Hank responded.

"Are those your headlights on the road coming in?" Bubba asked.

"Not us," Hank said. "From our vantage point, that group appears to be the cartel. There are a couple of moving vans and four trucks loaded with men carrying guns in the back."

"How many with you?" Stone asked.

"An even dozen," Hank responded.

"That leaves us at least two to one odds," Stone noted.

"We've had worse odds," Hank said.

"If you're not on the road coming in, are you coming in cross country?" Carter asked.

"You could say that." Hank chuckled. "Look up."

Carter's gaze shot to the sky, where dark silhouettes suspended from parachute canopies floated silently down to the ground outside the perimeter Stone's team had established.

As soon as they were down, the men gathered their silks and weighed them down to keep them from floating away on a gust of wind and warning the cartel of the team's existence at their transfer site.

Hank and his men moved into position with Stone's.

"Once the cartel starts the transfer, let them leave, then we'll move in," Hank said. "Remember, this isn't a third-world country. We would prefer to take them down, not kill them."

Carter's fingers tightened around the AR-15 rifle he'd chosen to take with him. "Don't we want to stop the cartel as well?"

"Yes, we do," Stone said. "That's where the DEA contingent headed this way by road will do their thing off the reservation. They'll be in position to capture the cartel once they leave the reservation."

"Don't we have to get permission from the tribal

council to conduct operations on the rez?" Moe's voice cut in.

"We have it," Hank said. "However, they didn't want us to take down the cartel on the rez. They wanted us to bring in the Native Americans running drugs on the reservation. They like cleaning up their own mess."

"Looks like everyone is here," Bubba said from the road.

"Not everyone," Carter said. "I haven't seen Nighthawk, Trevor, Colt or Eddie. Most importantly...I haven't seen Amanda or Tara."

"Incoming helicopter," Moe called out softly.

A helicopter like the one Carter had seen land on top of the casino flew into the transfer site and landed not far from where Carter lay flat against the earth.

A man wearing a suit stepped out.

"That's Nighthawk," Carter said, anger surging. He had to fight the urge to fire on the man and take his sorry ass out. A man from the Mexican cartel's lead vehicle stepped down from a black SUV and strode toward Nighthawk. Nighthawk handed him a satchel. Then the cartel leader turned and motioned for the transfer to begin.

While the gang members moved the drugs from one van to another, the armed cartel stood guard, weapons at the ready.

They worked quickly until all the product had

been transferred. Then the cartel members loaded into their trucks and drove back to the highway.

"Let's hope the Feds don't screw this up," Dax said. "They need to take out the people responsible for supplying the folks on the reservation."

"I still don't see Amanda or Tara," Carter said.

"I think I see someone inside the helicopter," Stone said. "Yes, I see the two missing women. One seems to be trying to get out of the chopper."

A figure fell out of the helicopter onto the ground. She sat up and shook long black hair out of her face.

Carter's heart soared. "It's Amanda."

Eddie Black Bear, aka Ernest Perez, jumped out behind her and jerked her to her feet. She swayed and almost fell. It appeared she was bound at the ankles.

The DEA agent slipped his arm around her waist and shouted to Nighthawk, "Let's go!"

"We can't let them leave with the women," Carter said softly.

"You're right," Hank said. "It's party time. Let's move in and clean up. Remember, we're not in the Middle East. Don't shoot unless you're fired on first."

Carter clenched his teeth. The don't-shoot order tied their hands, making it more difficult and dangerous to do their jobs.

He didn't care as long as he got Amanda out alive.

Ahead of him, Trevor Spotted Elk went toe-to-toe

with Colt Kickingwoman in a testosterone-laden strut of domination. They'd both taken chances coming there that night. They both wanted to leave with the largest portion of the take.

Colt motioned to one of his guys. "Take all of the product."

"What do you mean?" Trevor demanded. "Half of it is ours to distribute."

"I meant exactly what I said." Again, to his men standing behind him, he ordered. "Take it all."

Trevor frowned toward Theo. "What the fuck?"

Theo's brow dipped to form a V. "I didn't give that order."

"I did," Perez said. "Trevor broke the code. He and his people know the cost." He jerked his head toward Colt.

Colt pulled a handgun from beneath his jacket and shot Trevor.

"Things just got messy," Stone said. "Carter, Dax, Moe—go for the helicopter."

"Don't let it leave the ground with Amanda and Tara," Carter said. He gave up his prone position and raced for the helicopter. He had to get to her before Perez used her as a human shield or bargaining chip to get him out of Wyoming and the country altogether.

More shots rang out. Carter didn't look over his shoulder to see who was shooting whom. His focus zeroed in on Amanda.

CHAPTER 16

AMANDA HAD SPENT the day trying to work her hands out of the zip-tie to no avail. If they'd tied them in front, she could have used the same technique she'd used to break the duct tape.

Instead, she and Tara had taken turns trying to bite through the ties with no success.

About the time Tara had thought she was getting close to breaking through the plastic around Amanda's wrists, men showed up and drove the van out of the warehouse into the night.

They didn't have far to go, finally pulling into a well-lit area.

From her position on the van floor, Amanda couldn't see much until a neon sign appeared.

They were at the casino near Riverton.

She wanted to yell and scream to get someone's

attention, but she didn't want the wad of cloth shoved into her mouth again.

Conserving her strength and focus, she twisted her wrists again and again in an attempt to finish what Tara had started.

The van was parked in an underground parking garage. One of her guards opened the sliding door and stepped out. He reached in, grabbed Amanda's bound ankles and yanked her to the edge of the doorframe.

Amanda bunched her legs and kicked out as hard as she could, hitting the guy in the knees.

He yelled and bent over, clutching at his knees. "Bitch," he said and backhanded her across the cheek.

Amanda didn't have a chance to kick again. The man flung her over his shoulder, tossed her into a rolling laundry cart and threw a sheet over her head.

Tara yelled and cursed as they loaded her into the empty cart beside Amanda.

They were wheeled into an elevator.

Amanda couldn't tell how many floors they rose to, but when the doors opened, she could hear the sounds of traffic and felt a gentle breeze stir the sheet over her head.

She worked her wrists back and forth. The skin beneath the zip-tie had rubbed raw. Getting free was her goal, whatever it took.

The thumping sound of helicopter blades sounded

in the distance, growing closer until the roar of the engines filled Amanda's ears, and the downdraft of the rotors plastered the sheet against her face.

They had to be on top of the casino. A helicopter landed near them, the blades continuing to turn.

Her cart jerked and then rolled toward the roaring engine, the wind whipping the sheet from her face. Two men grabbed her beneath the arms and tossed her onto the helicopter floor next to Tara.

They wheeled the carts away, ducking beneath the spinning rotors.

Two men emerged from the building and hurried toward the chopper—Theo Nighthawk and Eddie Black Bear. They climbed aboard the helicopter, buckled themselves in and slipped headsets over their ears. The men on the rooftop closed the side doors, and the aircraft rose into the air.

There was no use yelling at the men to let her go. They wouldn't hear her voice over the engine or through their noise-canceling headsets.

Amanda continued to twist her wrists, praying the plastic would eventually break. She wouldn't get very far with the zip-ties around her ankles. Without anything sharp, she couldn't remove them and make a run for it. Still, she couldn't give up.

In the little bit of light from the helicopter control panel and the starlight shining through the windows, Amanda could tell the men were talking into their mikes, their brows low, their faces tight. She surmised it was getting close to midnight and the drug transfer.

Hope dared to swell in her chest. Carter and his team would be there. Hopefully, Hank Patterson would have called in some favors and sent more men to help clinch the operation.

Not long after they were airborne, the chopper slowed, hovered and then lowered to the ground.

Amanda's heart pounded against her chest—or was it the rumble of the aircraft engine vibrating through her?

The helicopter doors slid open. Nighthawk stepped out.

Amanda could see past them to the collection of vehicles and people gathered in an open area. If she hoped to get out of there alive, she had to make her move.

She watched as a man handed Nighthawk a satchel. Eddie was watching the exchange as well, his attention diverted from the women on the floor of the helicopter.

Amanda rolled to the edge of the door and fell out onto the ground, landing hard on her shoulder. Pain ripped through her, but she didn't let it stop her. Bunching her muscles, she prepared to roll away from the chopper.

She hadn't gotten anywhere before Eddie dropped down beside her and jerked her up by her hair.

"Let's go," he said.

In front of them, Trevor Spotted Elk and another man with many tattoos started a shouting match, surrounded by what Amanda assumed were the members of their respective gangs.

Then the man shouting at Trevor pulled a gun and shot Trevor.

All hell broke loose as the two teams fought. Some fired weapons; others engaged in hand-to-hand combat with knives, hatchets or machetes.

On the far side of the fray, Amanda caught sight of Nina Sweetwater and two other teens slipping into a car and driving away.

Good for them, she thought.

Nighthawk hurried toward Eddie and Amanda. "Let's get out of here. They have the drugs. They can figure out the distribution or kill themselves fighting. We don't care." He held up the satchel.

Eddie nodded. "That's right. We have what we came for. That and some insurance policies." His arm tightened around her waist. "Get into the chopper.

"No," Amanda said.

Eddie pulled a gun and held it to her head. "Get in or die."

"I'm your insurance policy, remember?" she taunted.

"I have another. I don't need you." His lip curled up on one corner, and his eyes narrowed.

The bastard was going to shoot her.

Amanda did the only thing she could do. She went limp.

With only one arm around her, Eddie couldn't hold her up and maintain his aim.

She slid down his side to the ground.

"Let her go," Nighthawk shouted. "We don't need her."

Eddie aimed at Amanda. "No, I don't. And I don't need you." He swung his gun around and shot Nighthawk in the face.

Nighthawk dropped where he stood, his hand still wrapped around the satchel handle.

Eddie turned to shoot Amanda next, but he'd barely raised his arm when he pitched forward and fell to his knees, the gun skittering across the ground in front of him.

Tara lay on the ground behind him, having rolled out of the helicopter with perfect timing.

"Are you all right?" Amanda called out.

"Yes," she said.

Eddie grabbed the gun, rolled to his feet and aimed at Amanda.

A shot rang out. Eddie reeled backward, tripped and fell to the ground, the gun flying well out of his reach.

The helicopter started to lift from the ground.

Eddie cried out, "No!" He crawled across the ground and grabbed for the satchel but had to pry it loose from Nighthawk's death grip. Once he had it in his good hand, he ran for the helicopter, tossed the satchel inside and threw himself at the open door. He landed on his belly, halfway in, his legs dangling.

Amanda tried to get up but couldn't.

Eddie was going to get away with murder. That couldn't happen.

A man emerged out of the darkness and dropped down beside her. "Amanda, are you okay?"

She almost cried her relief at the sound of Carter's voice. "Yes, but don't worry about us. You can't let Eddie get away."

He nodded and ran after the helicopter hovering a few feet off the ground with Eddie trying to get his leg up over the side. Eddie managed to get in and sprawl across the floor.

Carter took a flying leap, grabbed the edge of the open door and pulled himself into the aircraft.

Amanda's heart skipped several beats as the helicopter climbed higher.

Shouts and gunfire filled the air as the gangs continued to fight.

Another man dressed in combat gear and carrying a military-grade rifle dropped down beside her. In the starlight, she could see his face and recognized him as one of Carter's team from West Yellowstone. The man they'd called Moe.

"Stay down," he said. "Those bullets are real." He pulled out a wicked-looking knife and sliced through the zip-ties around her wrists and ankles.

Another one of Carter's team worked on freeing Tara.

The helicopter soon became only a blinking light in the sky.

Amanda and Tara lay low to the ground as more men dressed in combat gear moved in to surround what was left of the gangs.

"How did you get so many people here so fast?" Amanda asked.

"Hank Patterson has connections," Moe said.

As Hank's men rounded up the gang members, Wind River and Bureau of Indian Affairs Police vehicles rolled in, lights flashing. Behind them were ambulances, first responder vehicles and a couple of buses from the boys and girls club.

"You weren't kidding about Hank having connections," Amanda said. Her gaze went to the sky. The blinking light of the helicopter had disappeared. "Does he have connections in the sky?"

Moe laughed. "I think so. That's how he and his bunch from Eagle Rock got here." His smile slipped. "Don't worry. Carter will make it back."

An hour later, after the ambulances and buses left loaded with gang members, another set of vans arrived to take the Brotherhood Protectors home.

Hank Patterson found Amanda and Tara and introduced himself. "Glad to meet you two. I've heard a lot about you both." He nodded to Amanda. "Carter wanted me to let you know he made it safely to Casper, where he finally got the helicopter pilot to turn himself in."

Amanda let go of a huge sigh. "Thank you. And Eddie?"

"Eddie Back Bear, who is actually DEA agent Ernest Perez, was wounded. He didn't put up much of a fight before he passed out. He was taken into custody at the Casper Airport by a Federal Marshall and will be prosecuted for drug trafficking, money laundering and at least four counts of murder."

"He was the one who killed the teens," Amanda said.

"Along with his partner in crime, Theo Nighthawk," Hank said. "Their plan, based on the pilot's confession, was to take the money they were supposed to launder for the cartel, fly from here to Canada and take a plane to Cuba and disappear. Apparently, Perez and Nighthawk had been laundering money through the casino. The cartel pressured them to dump a massive amount of drugs onto the reservation. Perez figured their laundering days would be over if they were caught managing the drugs. He wanted out. They were going to take the money and run. Only he was greedy and wanted it all for himself."

"Money and drugs." Amanda shook her head. She hated that she hadn't been able to save the three teens who'd lost their lives. She wrapped an arm around

Tara and pulled her close. "I'm so sorry about Tobi. But I'm glad you and your family are now safe."

Tara nodded. "I'm going to talk my mother into moving to Bozeman or Spokane. We should be able to find work there. I don't want to stay where there are many reminders of Tobi and how he died."

"I don't blame you. I'll miss you." She hugged Tara.

"Thank you for fighting for the truth even when it put you in danger. It's nice to know people care about what happens to our people," Tara said.

Hank waved toward an SUV. "If you two are ready, we'll take you back to the hotel at Fort Washakie. Carter said he'd meet you there. He should be there shortly after we arrive."

"I'm ready." Amanda was eager to get back to town and even more anxious to see Carter.

"My team will stay the night in Fort Washakie and meet with authorities tomorrow to answer any questions before we head home."

Stone Jacobs joined them. "And I'll take Tara to be reunited with her family in West Yellowstone. Carter can follow us since his job is done here."

Amanda had been so concerned about stopping the killings and drug trafficking that she hadn't thought past that.

Stone was right. Carter had been hired to help keep her safe and find the murderer. Now that they'd accomplished both, Amanda didn't need Carter's services anymore.

But she still needed Carter. No. She wanted Carter. As crazy as it seemed, in the short time she'd known him, she'd allowed herself to fall in love. Now, she couldn't imagine life without him.

She climbed into the SUV, looking forward to seeing Carter, yet depressed that it might be the last time they'd be together.

CARTER BROKE every speed limit from Casper to Fort Washakie, Wyoming, just to get back to Amanda and see for himself that she was alive and well.

The hours he'd spent waiting for the battle to begin, waiting for Hank to arrive, and waiting to find out if Amanda was alive or dead had nearly killed him. He wanted to be with Amanda every day and night for the rest of his life, and he couldn't wait to tell her.

If she wasn't as like-minded, he'd spend however long it took to convince her to feel the same.

Hank had let him know they were staying at the hotel in Fort Washakie. Carter rented a car at the Casper airport and drove without stopping all the way back, pulling into the parking lot in the early hours of the morning. As soon as he stepped through the doors into the lobby, Amanda fell into his arms and hugged him around the waist so tightly he could barely breathe.

And he loved it.

He loved her.

He hugged her back, lifted her and spun her around before setting her back on her feet. Then he kissed her long and hard, only coming up when they both needed to catch their breath.

"I was so worried about you," he whispered. "I had one job. To keep you safe. And I failed."

"You didn't fail. You had to get Keme out of that hotel."

"That hotel didn't burn."

"It might have." She brushed her lips across his. "The point is, we survived, and now your job is done." She looked up into his eyes. "You can go back to West Yellowstone."

Carter frowned. "Do you want me to go back?"

She laughed. "Hell, no. I want you to stay with me forever. But I would never ask you to give up your job to stay here where there are so few places to work, rampant poverty and substance abuse."

He grinned. "Sounds like heaven—as long as I'm with you." He brushed a strand of her silky black hair back behind her ear. "I never thought I'd say this again... I'm in love."

She stared up into his eyes, her brow wrinkling. "I thought you never wanted to love again."

"I didn't want to," he said. "You came along with

all of your passion for helping others and those beautiful blue eyes. I didn't have a choice. My heart chose you." He cupped her cheeks and stared down into her eyes. "And I don't have to give up my job. I might have to be away from time to time, but I'll always come home to you."

She smiled up into his eyes. "I've never heard sweeter words. I love you, Carter Manning."

"I love you, Amanda Small."

EPILOGUE

Two months later...

"Thank you for coming all the way over to Eagle Rock for this celebration." Sadie McClain Patterson took the insulated casserole dish from Amanda's hands and smiled at her and Carter. "Hank was glad to hear you two would make it. He's so proud of all the good work his team of Brotherhood Protectors has accomplished. This little celebration is just a small way to thank you all."

"Brotherhood Protectors wouldn't exist if not for the brave men who chose to join us." Hank joined Sadie on the front porch. "Come in. The others are out back, waiting for Bear to finish grilling the steaks."

"I could smell them as soon as we got out of the car," Carter said.

Amanda's stomach rumbled and she laughed. "Me, too."

"The steaks are from our own grass-fed Angus, raised on the ranch." Hank held the door open. "Come meet some of the guys who came down for operation Wind River Reclamation."

Amanda smiled. "Is that what you called it?"

Hank shrugged. "Not really, but it sounded good. Hopefully, catching the gangs in the act of receiving drugs and shooting each other will help to keep them behind bars."

"The tribal council is asking for assistance from the federal government to help rehabilitate and reskill the less violent young people to make them more productive contributors to the community," Amanda said. "We know we can't eradicate drug and alcohol abuse, but if we keep them busy and gainfully employed, we won't have as big a problem."

"Treating the root of the problem, not the symptoms." Hank nodded. "Good thinking."

He let them through the massive living room with a stone fireplace that stretched from the floor to the ceiling.

Out on the back porch and lawn was a crowd of people. A couple of guys threw a football. Some of the men and women were hitting a volleyball back and forth across a net.

Laughter and conversation filled the air.

Hank took Carter and Amanda around, introducing them to men named Swede, Bear, Duke, Kujo, Taz, Boomer, Viper, Chuck, Gavin, Maddog and so many more. Not to mention each of the men had a fiancée or wife.

Amanda lost track of who was who, but they all made her feel welcome and at home.

"How's working from Fort Washakie working out for you?" Swede asked.

"I'm away from home a lot, but when I'm back, it's great being with Amanda." He touched a hand to her back and smiled down at her.

Stone and Kyla joined them on the porch. "Did you tell Hank the good news?" Kyla asked.

Hank's brow wrinkled. "Good news?"

Carter frowned and shook his head. "No, not yet."

Amanda looked at Carter as color rose up his neck. "What good news?"

Kyla touched a hand to her mouth. "Oops. Sorry. I thought you'd already… Sorry."

Her frown deepening, Amanda looked from Kyla to Stone and back to Carter. "What news?"

"It's not actually news yet," Carter said. "Not until this." He held up the diamond ring Amanda had borrowed from Kyla for their fake engagement.

He dropped to one knee and held out the ring. "I bought this ring from Kyla because I believe it brought you and me together from the moment we slid it onto your finger."

He held it out to her. "Amanda Small, would you do me the honor of being my real fiancée? And, please, marry me at your earliest convenience because I don't think I can live another day without you in my life."

Tears welled in Amanda's eyes and slipped down her cheeks. "Oh, Carter."

He frowned. "The question requires a yes or no answer. Not an 'Oh-Carter.'" He shook his head. "You're killing me, Small."

She laughed and nodded. "Yes. A million times, yes!"

He rose, slipped the beautiful ring on her finger and crushed her into his arms.

Amanda's heart filled with joy as she held the man of her dreams in her arms, with the ring she'd grown to love on her finger. She couldn't wait to get back to Wind River to tell Joe. He already loved Carter like a son.

"Oh," Carter said. "I already cleared it with Joe. He gave me permission to ask for your hand. He also told me to tell you to say yes."

Amanda flung her arms around his neck and held on tightly. "I'm the luckiest girl in the world. I have you."

"I'm the luckiest man in the world to have you in my life." He hugged her once more and then set her at arm's length. "We might have gotten it backwards by putting the ring on your finger before falling in love, but it worked out."

She smiled down at the ring that had brought them together. "Yes, it did. And I wouldn't change a thing about the way you and I came to be us."

Interested in more military romance stories?
Subscribe to my newsletter and receive the Military Heroes Box Set
Subscribe Here

SAVING LILIANA

BROTHERHOOD PROTECTORS
YELLOWSTONE BOOK #3

New York Times & USA Today
Bestselling Author

ELLE JAMES

YELLOWSTONE
SAVING LILIANA

BROTHERHOOD PROTECTORS

New York Times & USA Today Bestselling Author
ELLE JAMES

ABOUT SAVING LILIANA

ABANDONED BY HIS MOTHER, raised by a taciturn Marine, Dax joined the Navy to become a SEAL. Fast-forward twelve years later, he's out of the navy, done time as a mercenary and now works for Brotherhood Protectors. Never trusted women. Never married. Never wanted to.

Lawyer and motivational speaker, Liliana Lightfeather is running for the US house of representatives for the state of Wyoming. From the Wind River Reservation, she clawed her way out of poverty to become a lawyer representing her people and the rest of Wyoming.

After attempts on her life, she turns to the Brotherhood Protectors Yellowstone to see her through her campaign. Expecting an older woman as his assignment, Dax is disturbed to find she's not old and very pretty. Thankfully, he's immune to love...until he gets a taste of the woman's passion. Dax fights unknown threats to keep her alive and in the process falls victim to the curse of love.

Saving Liliana

SEAL SALVATION

BROTHERHOOD PROTECTORS
COLORADO BOOK #1

New York Times & *USA Today*
Bestselling Author

ELLE JAMES

SEAL SALVATION

BROTHERHOOD PROTECTORS
Colorado

New York Times & USA Today Bestselling Author

ELLE JAMES

PROLOGUE

Hank Patterson paced the length of the conference table in the basement of his home in Montana, muttering, "No man left behind."

"Hey, boss." Axel Svenson, the giant of a Viking, ducked as he descended the steps into the headquarters of one of the finest security firms in the state of Montana.

Hank, a former Navy SEAL, had started the Brotherhood Protectors after he'd rescued movie star Sadie McClain when her bodyguards were less than effective. Since then, he'd married the movie star, had a couple of kids and hired a number of former Army, Navy and Marine special operations, highly-trained operatives, to provide security or conduct dangerous missions where the government wasn't or couldn't get involved.

He took pride in the fact he'd helped so many of

his military brotherhood find a place to fit into the civilian world.

With a large contingent of his men based in Montana, he needed to create other bases of operations. He'd set up an office in Hawaii, where former SEAL Jace "Hawk" Hawkins was the only man currently handling business there. He and some of his men had discussed other locations, including Washington, DC, New Orleans, Atlanta, New York City and Colorado.

Having grown up on a ranch, Hank liked the idea of setting up another location in an area much like his beloved Montana. Now, all he needed was to find the men to run the location.

"Hey, Hank," a familiar voice sounded from the staircase. "What's up?"

Hank lifted his chin toward Joseph "Kujo" Kuntz. "Sorry to take you away from your family on a Sunday."

Kujo descended the stairs, followed by his retired Military Working Dog, Six. "No problem. Molly had to go to her office in Bozeman to pick up some files and check in with her supervisor."

Hank smiled. "How's the pregnancy going?"

Kujo shoved a hand through his hair. "First three months were a bitch with morning sickness, but she's feeling good now."

"Will she continue to work for the FBI after the baby is born?" Hank asked.

Kujo's lips twisted, and his brow dipped. "Much as I'd like her to quit and raise our baby, it wouldn't be fair to ask her to do that. She's good at her job."

"And you and Six are good at yours." Hank's brow rose. "You're not considering quitting, are you?"

Kujo laughed. "No way. But we're in the process of interviewing nannies."

Hank nodded. "Glad to hear it. You're a vital member of the team, here."

"Thanks," Kujo said. "I'm sure you didn't invite me here to ask about morning sickness and babies. You've got your hands full with your own children, one of which is a newborn, probably keeping you awake at night."

"Truth." Hank's smile slipped. "Think you can get away for a couple weeks before the baby is born?"

Kujo nodded slowly. "Where did you have in mind?"

Hank nodded his head toward the white board on the wall where a computer image of a state was projected. "I've got a lead on a location for our new office."

Kujo stepped closer. "New office? Where?"

"Your old stomping grounds," Hank said. "Colorado."

A grin spread across Kujo's face. "That's great." As soon as the grin came it faded. "Only, I can't be gone for long with Molly being pregnant."

Hank nodded. "I don't want you to move out

there permanently. I just need you to get out there, set up shop and hire a few good men, keeping in mind that one of them will head up the location."

"I hate to be gone so long from Molly," Kujo said. "If it's okay with her, I can give you a few weeks. She's only four months along, which gives me a little time that I can be away."

"I wanted to be with Sadie every day of her pregnancy," Hank said.

"I'd like to be with Molly every day of hers. But if you need me to go to Colorado, now would be better than later this year."

Hank nodded. "Good. And I have someone in mind for leading the new team out there." His brow wrinkled. "Only he's a work in progress."

Kujo frowned. "What do you mean...work in progress?"

Hank sighed. "Not only has he lost a leg, he's lost his way."

Kujo's eyes narrowed. "I can understand. I was at my lowest when you offered me a job. If it hadn't been for you and the Brotherhood Protectors..." Kujo shook his head, his hand going automatically to Six's head.

The dog nuzzled his fingers, sensing his handler's emotions.

"I figured you of all people would see where I'm going with this. And you're from Colorado. You'll appreciate going back."

Kujo ran a hand over Six's smooth, sable head. "You saved my life, and Six's, not long ago," Kujo said quietly.

"You and Six were worth saving. And so is Jake Cogburn."

Kujo's eyes widened. "Jake 'The Cog' Cogburn?"

Hank nodded again. "He's in a bad way, from what I hear."

"Like I was when you found me and made me rescue Six?"

"Exactly. I figured you'd have a better connection with the SEAL."

Kujo drew in a deep breath. "He has to be ready to make the change."

Hank laughed. "And you were?"

Kujo grinned. "I wasn't. But you were convincing. And knowing Six would be euthanized if I didn't go to him, motivated me."

"Cog needs someone to motivate him," Hank said. "He needs a purpose. He needs to know he's still relevant in this world."

"And you think I'm the man to pull him up by his bootstraps?" Kujo shook his head. "I don't know. Might take more than the few weeks I can give to the job."

Hank clapped Kujo on the back. "I've seen your work. I know you can handle it."

"And you want me to set up a new office for the Brotherhood Protectors?" Kujo shook his head.

"That, in itself, will take some time. I'll have to find a building to rent or purchase and equip it with all the infrastructure needed." He waved his hand at Hank's basement. "This takes time."

"I have a connection near Colorado Springs." Hank turned and walked away. "He's a former Marine gunnery sergeant running a dude ranch near a small town called Fool's Gold, which is located outside of Colorado Springs." He touched several keys on a computer keyboard, and an image popped up on a screen.

Kujo looked over Hank's shoulder to view a map on the monitor.

"I think Gunny Tate's ranch has everything we need to set up shop. Great location, private enough and they need the money we'd pay in rent. It's a win-win situation. Besides, the ranch will give us the cover we need to run our operations without detection."

"Kind of like what you have here." Kujo nodded. "We're just a bunch of ranch hands, until we're given an assignment."

"Exactly." Hank's grin widened. "Gunny Tate is a character. He raised his only child singlehandedly after his wife died in childbirth. I believe that child is grown now and working the dude ranch with him. Gunny is a blustery curmudgeon with a heart of gold. Met him at McP's a million years ago after BUD/S training. His team was celebrating his transfer to a recruiting command in Colorado. He's been in Colorado ever since."

"Recruiting command?" Kujo's brows rose. "Who'd he piss off?"

Hank shook his head. "He opted to go into recruiting to end his career in a place of his choice. Being a single father raising a child, when he could be deployed at a moment's notice, wore on him. He wanted to slow down and give the child a steady home to grow up in."

"Boy or girl?" Kujo asked.

Hank grinned. "Name's Rucker. Trust Gunny to give him a tough name. I can only assume he's a boy. I never had the pleasure of meeting him."

Kujo drew in a deep breath, let it out and clapped his hands together. "When do you want me to go? This week? Next week? You name it."

Hank picked up a sheet of paper off the printer beside the monitor. "Your plane leaves at six in the morning from Bozeman and arrives in Colorado Springs before noon. That should give you plenty of time to find the town of Fool's Gold and Lost Valley Ranch. Gunny is expecting you and will take you to where Cogburn is holed up."

Kujo leaned his head toward the German Shepherd lying patiently at his feet. "What about Six?"

Hank smiled. "If you want, I can book him in the seat beside yours on the airplane."

Kujo glanced down at Six. "Guess I'm going home to Colorado. I'd like Six to stay here with Molly."

Six rose to his feet. Ready to go.

"Sorry, boy," Kujo said. "You're needed here."

Hank held out his hand. "Good luck convincing Cog we have a place for him. He was a helluva SEAL and a leader among his team. If you can pull him out of his funk, he'll make a great team leader for our Colorado location. That is, unless you'd like to take that position…?" Hank raised his eyebrows.

Kujo shook his head. "Molly's established herself at the Bozeman office of the FBI. They know her and what she's capable of. With her being pregnant, it would be a bad time to move. She'd have to start all over making her mark."

Hank nodded. "Figured as much. Besides, she has a great support system here to take care of your baby when you're both called to duty."

"Exactly. I wouldn't ask her to move now. Maybe in a year or two, but not now. I do miss Colorado. Fortunately, Montana is a lot like where I came from. Wide open spaces, blue sky, mountains and more. Here, I have a team I love working with." He shook Hank's hand. "Thanks for pulling me back into the land of the living."

"You're welcome. Now go get Cog. I have a feeling he'll be just the right fit for running the Colorado office of the Brotherhood Protectors."

As Kujo and Six left the basement conference

room, Hank's gaze followed. If anyone could get Jake Cogburn to pull his head out of his ass and get to work, Kujo was the one.

"Hank?" Sadie's voice sounded from the top of the stairs.

"Yeah, babe," he responded, taking the stairs two at a time.

His beautiful wife stood with baby Mac cradled in her arms.

Hank leaned close and captured her mouth with his. "What's up, beautiful?"

She kissed him back and smiled up at him. "Is Kujo going to Colorado?"

Hank nodded. "He is."

Sadie nodded. "I'm glad. If I didn't have to show up on the set of my next film, you could go." She frowned. "I could call and reschedule."

"Don't. Kujo can handle Cog." He kissed Sadie again. "Besides, I'm looking forward to having Mac and Emma all to myself while I miss their mama."

Sadie's smile spread across her face. "I love you, Hank Patterson. And I love that you care about your former teammates enough to help them out."

He leaned back, raising his eyebrows. "Are you kidding? They're helping me. I couldn't have built this business so big and so fast without them."

Hank took Mac from Sadie's arms and carried him into the living room where Emma played with her collection of stuffed animals spread out across the area rug.

He prayed Cogburn wouldn't send Kujo packing. The man really needed a purpose for his life. If he had that, he'd realize that being short a leg wasn't the end of the world.

ABOUT THE AUTHOR

ELLE JAMES also writing as MYLA JACKSON is a *New York Times* and *USA Today* Bestselling author of books including cowboys, intrigues and paranormal adventures that keep her readers on the edges of their seats. When she's not at her computer, she's traveling, snow skiing, boating, or riding her ATV, dreaming up new stories. Learn more about Elle James at www.ellejames.com

Website | Facebook | Twitter | GoodReads | Newsletter | BookBub | Amazon

Or visit her alter ego Myla Jackson at mylajackson.com
Website | Facebook | Twitter | Newsletter

Follow Me!
www.ellejames.com
ellejamesauthor@gmail.com

Tactical Force (#5)

Disruptive Force (#6)

Mission: Six

One Intrepid SEAL

Two Dauntless Hearts

Three Courageous Words

Four Relentless Days

Five Ways to Surrender

Six Minutes to Midnight

Hearts & Heroes Series

Wyatt's War (#1)

Mack's Witness (#2)

Ronin's Return (#3)

Sam's Surrender (#4)

Take No Prisoners Series

SEAL's Honor (#1)

SEAL'S Desire (#2)

SEAL's Embrace (#3)

SEAL's Obsession (#4)

SEAL's Proposal (#5)

SEAL's Seduction (#6)

SEAL'S Defiance (#7)

Hot Velocity (#4)

Cajun Magic Mystery Series

Voodoo on the Bayou (#1)

Voodoo for Two (#2)

Deja Voodoo (#3)

Cajun Magic Mysteries Books 1-3

SEAL Of My Own

Navy SEAL Survival

Navy SEAL Captive

Navy SEAL To Die For

Navy SEAL Six Pack

Devil's Shroud Series

Deadly Reckoning (#1)

Deadly Engagement (#2)

Deadly Liaisons (#3)

Deadly Allure (#4)

Deadly Obsession (#5)

Deadly Fall (#6)

Covert Cowboys Inc Series

Triggered (#1)

Taking Aim (#2)

Bodyguard Under Fire (#3)

Baby Bling

Under Suspicion, With Child

Texas-Size Secrets

Cowboy Sanctuary

Lakota Baby

Dakota Meltdown

Beneath the Texas Moon

Made in the USA
Las Vegas, NV
23 September 2022

55815402R10174